About the Author

My passion has always been in education, from running a performing arts school in Dubai to being a specialist SEN tutor. I help children from all walks of life develop and hone skills to not only pass exams but enable them to integrate into a sometimes-unforgiving society. I have always worked to ensure all children had access to their education and their best selves. I champion every single child I work with in order to give them a voice. Being fifty-five now, it's time for me to shine.

Telford Parade

Kim Valentine

Telford Parade

Vanguard Press

VANGUARD PAPERBACK

© Copyright 2024
Kim Valentine

A CIP catalogue record for this title is
available from the British Library.

ISBN 978 1 80016 894 7

*Vanguard Press is an imprint of
Pegasus Elliot Mackenzie Publishers Ltd.*
www.pegasuspublishers.com

First Published in 2024

**Vanguard Press
Sheraton House Castle Park
Cambridge England**

Printed & Bound in Great Britain

Dedication

Dedicated to my dear friends, Ginny, Lisa, Belinda and of course John. You believed in me and gave me the strength to write. My gratitude is unfathomable.

Acknowledgements

Bobbie, for your continuous encouragement and belief
in me.

Chapter 1

For the first time in a long time, Suzie had a day off. Slipping out of bed as quietly as she could, so as not to disturb Max, she headed for her beloved Queen Anne chair. Its vantage point, just by the window, allowed her a glimpse into another world, far removed from her own. The people she watched never knowing her eyes were on them, all the while wondering to herself where they were coming from and going to. The endless possibilities ran through her mind like a showreel at the beginning of the main feature.

The young couple, so intent on their own conversation and thoughts. Holding hands as if life would end if they ever let go. A well-dressed gentleman, his tweed coat swaying like a vast wave in the wind as he walked. His purpose she didn't know, but he was striding to the beat of his own life. The huddle of schoolgirls at the bus stop, laughing and joking about boys and their first loves, no doubt. *Where did that feeling go?* Suzie thought to herself, remembering with fondness her first love and how very precious it was. Lost forever but never forgotten.

Pondering her life, all thoughts of the passers-by gone for now, she thought of her much-loved business; Crichton's was Suzie's baby. After leaving uni she took an internship with Catherine Walker for a while, but her desire to create her own brand was too much. So, like all other hopefuls at the time, she ploughed every spare penny into a tiny little studio right at the top of an old Victorian block in Covent Garden. Along with her friends Gina and Kelly, the three of them felt right at home scribbling their designs by day and sewing into the early hours of the morning.

Never feeling the need to change her name after marrying Max, Suzie was proud of her achievement and nobody could take that away from her. But there was always something missing. Since she was a little girl, she had pictured herself in a rural setting with a couple of kids and a dog. She could imagine the house perfectly. Filled with the sound of children's laughter as they gently played amongst the flowers. The dog barking happily and life feeling complete. Thinking about it now just made her giggle a little. *Straight out of a Famous Five book*, she thought to herself.

As the radio came on, Suzie stretched herself and headed over to the bed. She couldn't help but smile at the loveliness of it all. The calmest greens were painted on the walls, entwined with the palest green and vanilla checks and a sumptuous cherry wood floor. All as specific to Suzie as any outfit she would ever design.

Max had been very quiet last night; she had sensed a while back that something was up, women's intuition they call it. After searching all his pockets and smelling his shirts for a week or so, she had tried to put the nagging feeling to the back of her mind. Her Mother had once told her, "If you feel the need to look, there is usually something to look for!"

Sliding herself back into bed, she snuggled up to Max, spooning him with her small frame. He was as warm as toast on a wintry day and very inviting.

"Time to get up, sleepyhead," she whispered into his ear. Landing tiny little kisses across his shoulders, she ran her fingers down the full length of his body. Was she imagining it, or had Max pulled away ever so slightly from her touch? Back in the day, he would yield to her, turning to face her, kissing her face and tickling her ribs. Not today, he just lay there, his back to her, his thoughts elsewhere. Pulling back the covers, he rose to his feet and headed for the bathroom. Striding with a new sense of purpose, Max knew he had to escape her prying eyes, for his would surely give away his feelings. By the time Suzie had showered and changed, he had left for work and the apartment was empty. Just Suzie and her thoughts remained.

Chapter 2

Pottering around the apartment, Suzie could hear her neighbours. They were arguing again. Well, Laura seemed to be doing most of the talking. Steven Sandgate and Laura Nelson lived next door at number three. Smiling at the thought of him, she remembered his broad shoulders and washboard stomach. *That must have taken endless hours in the gym,* she mused. With his wavy blond hair and tortoiseshell glasses, he looked every inch the lawyer. His crisp white shirts and flawless suits showed he meant business. She bet he was a pitbull in front of a jury. As for Laura, she was an aspiring actress whom Suzie had been trying to sign up for ages. She had the smallest face, almost elf-like, crowned with short auburn hair and such deep green eyes. The smattering of freckles across her nose meant she was impeccable. Their arguments seemed to have escalated over the past few weeks, and Suzie, for one, was getting a little tired of the constant bickering.

The phone rang, bringing her back to her senses, and from the caller ID, it was the agency. They wanted her input regarding a new model, so, she would have to go into work after all.

Deciding to take a taxi, she headed out into the cool morning, the sun just starting to burn the clouds away. It was going to be a nice day. If she played her cards right, she could get everything done by lunchtime and still get some shopping in before meeting Max.

Stepping into Crichton's at just past ten, Suzie was confronted with a very unhappy model who had just been signed by the agency. From the way she was bitching and moaning, it wasn't hard to see she didn't like the photographer assigned to her.

"Is this what you have called me in for on my day off?" Suzie asked.

"I know, I am really sorry, but we couldn't calm her down, and she would only speak to you, nobody else," Kelly said, her shrug of the shoulders and roll of the eyes an indication of her annoyance.

Kelly was thirty-two and by far one of Suzie's best friends. They had been together from the start, and Suzie couldn't imagine life without her. She knew everything that was needed and organised their days with precision.

Dealing as swiftly as she could with the newly signed Chloe Mallery, Suzie convinced her that she had the best photographer in London. This girl had a temper like no other. *She will have to rein that in if she wanted to stay signed to Crichton's,* Suzie thought to herself. Fortunately, it wasn't as bad as she imagined it would be. Once Chloe had cooled down and Suzie had convinced Peter, the photographer, to take his coat off and that she really was worth the angst, calm ensued. Reminding Kelly as she walked past her desk to drop something lovely in the post for Peter as an apology, she snatched up her own pile of post, put it into her Chanel tote, and with a wave to everyone, set off to do some shopping.

The shops were buzzing with tourists and lots of children. *It must be half-term or something,* Suzie thought to herself. The street entertainers were out in force, and the atmosphere was uplifting. Heading for the stall that she loved the most, Suzie stopped to chat to Amos. They had become firm friends over the years, and his sock stall had been featured many times in articles about Crichton's and their fashion shows. Holding up a pure paisley pair and a navy with green tartan, she asked his opinion for her dad. His birthday was approaching, and these were always a great staple if all else failed. They chatted as friends do, and Suzie relished in the glow that their friendship meant to her. Amos wasn't just a sock vendor; he was an intricate cog in Crichton's wheels.

As she walked away, Amos gave out a wolf whistle, making Suzie blush. Dressed in a cream Chanel suit and seeming to all that glanced in her direction that it took no effort to look that good, Suzie felt she could conquer the world. Turning to blow a kiss back to Amos, her face radiant in the glow of happiness, she could feel the stresses and strains of the last few months starting to drop away.

Deciding on a small café in the middle of the old market for lunch, she chose a table outside. The sun was shining and the sky was the bluest she had seen in weeks. She was looking forward to a little rest and relaxation, wanting to watch the world go by and lose herself in her fantasy world. Suzie knew this always made her feel better. After a club sandwich and light salad, the bottle of sparkling white wine she had ordered was now half full. It was time to settle back and enjoy the next couple of hours, preoccupying herself with wondering what he did for a living or where she was going. The game was a firm favourite as there were no winners.

Scanning her surroundings, Suzie finally looked straight into the eyes of a very handsome stranger. He was watching her intently, delighting in her facial expressions as she pondered what she saw. *Oh goodness, I hope he doesn't guess what I am doing,* she thought to herself as she noticed he was scribbling and drawing the whole time.

Feeling brave after her half bottle of wine, she smiled over at him. His first reaction was to look behind himself, in case she was looking at someone else. This made Suzie laugh, and he knew then that he wanted to meet her and needed to talk to this beautiful woman that he had watched for so long.

Suzie froze as she saw he was coming over. Dressed casually in a pair of Levi's and a checked shirt, its collar flapping as he walked, giving Suzie a glimpse of his chest. Reaching down, he placed the button back where it belonged; *it's always coming undone,* he thought to himself as he carried on walking. At least six feet two, she decided, compared to her five-foot frame, he was a giant. Feeling her stomach tie itself in knots, Suzie berated herself. After all, she dealt with people all day, and here she was worried about a stranger. The trouble was, he looked at her so intently she felt her soul being searched and was unsure how this made her feel.

Chapter 3

"Greg Samuels," he said stretching out his hand and smiling, his dark eyes shining as he did so.

"Hi, I'm Suzie Crichton," she said, feeling a little self-conscious even though she was dressed flawlessly. "Please, join me." She added, gesturing to the seat opposite. Her heart pounded just thinking about this beautiful stranger. Beckoning the waiter to bring another glass, she hadn't thought to ask Greg if he even wanted wine. He nodded and let her take the lead, realising he needed to get his wits about him to think of what to say now that he was in such close proximity and there was nowhere to hide.

They began tentatively to talk about work and what they did. Suzie found out that Greg was a writer, currently in the middle of a romance novel set in Ireland during the early part of the century. Intrigued by his profession, she wanted to read some of his work now, to see what he thought romance was.

"Unfortunately, I have been baking more than I have been writing this month," he said with a smile that lit up his whole face. "The block is engulfing me, and if it doesn't end soon, my editor is going to kill me."

Greg was impressed to find out that Suzie ran a large design house and modelling agency.

"I bet you are a force to be reckoned with in the boardroom," he said, making her laugh. She made light of his joke, but she knew that her hard work, and that of her team, was really paying off. Crichton's was going places, and she was so excited to see how it all panned out.

They talked and talked, and Suzie felt as if she had known him for years. They batted off each other with ease, and even the small silences were welcomed. *How easy it was,* Greg thought, *to actually meet someone and not a dating site to be found.*

Glancing at her watch, its tank design her favourite ever, a gift from Cartier many years before and still a firm favourite. She couldn't believe how fast the time had passed. Making her excuses, she beckoned for the bill and set about leaving.

Due at an art gallery at seven o'clock to meet Max. Suzie hated the thought of another night mingling with chinless wonders that bored her to death and weren't what she wanted or needed in her life right now. Oh, how she wished that she could take more control, just as she had in her business. Max, however, was convinced that by going out night after night she would soon forget that she wanted to have a family.

"Don't go," Greg said. "Sit a while longer, and I will order another bottle of wine, and we can carry on talking and getting to know each other." With that, a pang of guilt hit Suzie like a ton of bricks. She realised she hadn't mentioned Max the whole time or the fact that she was married.

"I can't, really," she said. "I have to meet my husband and we have an engagement to keep."

Greg looked mortified.

"I didn't realise that you were married. I'm really sorry; you never said, and I just assumed." Looking down at her ring finger now, the sudden realisation that she had left her wedding ring on the bathroom sink that morning made her smile. Suzie got up and made her apologies; she had to get away from this man. Leaving Greg dumbfounded, she almost ran across the market square and out of sight.

Supposing she would never see him again, she hailed a taxi to her beloved Telford Parade to get changed for the evening and ready for her night with Max. At the same time, Greg had gathered up his belongings and was now speeding towards his newly acquired apartment, in a lovely Art Deco block that he had loved as soon as he had seen it.

Telford Parade Mansions stood proudly on the corner of Parade Street. Built in 1930, symmetrical to a fault and three stories high.

As the two cars pulled up outside, Greg couldn't believe his eyes; Suzie was stepping out of her taxi. She looked like a small flower that had been blown about in the wind. Her cheeks happily flushed from the sparkling wine and the heart-stopping conversation she had enjoyed with a handsome stranger.

"Hi, what are you doing here?" She said with a little flutter of excitement.

"I could say the same to you," Greg said. "I live here, what's your excuse?"

"Me too," replied a now startled Suzie. "Apartment four, to be exact." She found out that Greg had just moved into apartment one. She had wondered who the new neighbour was but never in her wildest dreams would it have been Greg.

Walking in step as they entered the large lobby, Suzie couldn't even look at Greg. She was too scared. She didn't want him to see how happy he had made her feel in the last few hours.

Making his way to his new apartment, Greg heard her push the button for the lift. Its groaning motor awakened, and like a sleeping lion, it roared into action. She could use the stairs but was worried her legs would give way before she reached the next floor. As the lift came to a stop and the concertina gate had been firmly opened, Suzie prayed for him to speak — to tell her not to go. Chastising herself for her silly wish as she knew she couldn't carry this on with him, especially not here. Greg, taking one last look, opened his front door and stepped inside. The moment was gone. Suzie's heart felt heavy and sad, and at that very second, she knew that decisions had to be made. She wanted more and was tired of all Max's games.

Chapter 4

"Come on, Laura, we'll be late and miss the beginning of the show," Steven said as he stood in the doorway, tapping his keys for effect.

"Okay, just coming!" Laura yelled from the bathroom, giving her make-up one last check. She snatched up her bag and headed out to join him. They bumped into Suzie as they were going to get into the lift.

"Hi, you two, off somewhere nice?"

"Just an art gallery showing a friend's work. I am hoping to make some contacts," Laura said. Suzie was still reeling from lunch, so just wished them well and said they would have to catch up sometime soon.

Steven Sandgate turned heads wherever he went. Chiselled good looks and a charisma that followed him like an aura. A sensitive man who loved life and Laura, his girlfriend, always taking her hand and asking after her, making sure she was just right. To Laura, this was an endearing feature at the start but was quickly becoming a trait she least admired. How was she ever going to get her big break with him constantly on her heels?

Arriving at the art gallery was like a night at the Oscars. Laura was in her element, but for Steven, who hated the limelight, it was a step too far out of his comfort zone. In court, it was different; he knew what he was doing there. There were photographers everywhere, and it seemed as if every facet of their outfits were on display. The champagne was flowing, and for this, Laura was thankful. Snatching up two glasses, she handed one to Steven and started scanning the venue. After her friend had given her a sneaky peek at the guest list, she knew exactly who she wanted to meet: David Summers, so she had read, was one of the best-known television producers of modern times.

It was rumoured that he was on the lookout for his next big star: a lead for a new television series about a lady cop that was both glamorous and tough. Laura would fit the bill nicely, or so she thought. What she needed was to ditch Steven for a while; he would cramp her style if she came face to face with Summers. Introducing him to her friend Sonia, a fellow lawyer, she knew they would chat for hours given the right cues.

"Tell Steven about that case you are on at the moment, Sonia. It's been all over the tabloids, and I think this one will make you famous." With that, she turned on her heels and strode out into the party like a lioness looking for her prey.

Summers was, as usual, surrounded by a throng of women, all hanging off his every word and hoping that today would be the day that he noticed them. Laura had no such intentions. She was going to make him want her, and want her he did. As she passed him by, her auburn hair and green eyes caught him off guard. Laura had been warned about people offering her everything and giving her nothing, so was taking it all in her stride and making him work for it. Stepping out of the throng, he headed in her direction and soon found himself face to face with who he described later in a television interview as the next big thing! David was a very tactile man, and when he wanted something, he got it, and he was going to have her, there was no doubt in his mind.

Laura could feel him undressing her with his eyes and also his words. He told her how beautiful she was and how she could go far in television. As she stepped back away from him, he caught her wrist in his hand and tugged her towards him.

"I could make you a star," he said, raising his hand to touch her face. Stroking her cheek, his hand dropping, he tapped her gently on the behind. Laura laughed, throwing her head backwards, arching her back as if offering herself to him. She had seen this done many times at auditions and thought she would try it out. After all, she needed this break and didn't mind a little flirting to get it. Summers was enthralled; he wanted this girl, and by golly, he was going to have her!

Witnessing the whole scene, Steven was horrified to see another man's hands and eyes caressing his girlfriend. Why was she letting this happen? His sudden realisation that Laura really didn't care about him at all was like a punch to the chest. From his vantage point, he could see her playing with Summers, willing him to touch her, teasing him and leading him on. Maybe it was only just acting, but he had seen enough.

"Hello, Steven," Suzie said as she headed in his direction. Her eyes drawn to what was making him look angrier than she had ever seen him.

Sighing, she patted his arm as if to say, "I see what you see". There really weren't any words, so she just stood and waited. Why had Max told her she had to come tonight when he wasn't even here himself? The silence between them was palpable, and she needed to escape. There were no words she could say to appease Steven, so she didn't even try.

She might as well make the most of it and get a drink; her stomach was growling with hunger, so she headed towards the bar area to seek out a glass of bubbly and some appetizers.

Bumping straight into Laura as she came out of the bathroom, they both spluttered out apologies and then realised they knew each other.

"Hello, Laura, how are you? I'm looking for Max, have you seen him?"

Laura was preoccupied and just shrugged and said, "Sorry I have to find Steven; we'll catch up next week." At that point, Laura whisked off, and Suzie was left alone pondering whether to stay or go. She decided on the latter and didn't look back for Max or anything else. Her hunger could wait.

Steven, having decided to go and get himself a stiff drink, was sitting on a bar stool when Laura finally decided to find him. He was seething and wanted to have it out with her, but she was having none of it. Changing the subject, she wouldn't focus on anything Steven was saying.

"We need to get out of here Laura. Come on, let's go home," Steven said calmly, even though he didn't feel calm. His heart was pounding out of his chest, and he felt as though his world had fallen apart.

"I don't want to go home yet," Laura said and walked off in the direction of David Summers. She knew she wanted to work for him and now was the time to tell him. Tomorrow was too far away, and she needed to know where she stood before she could deal with Steven.

David Summers, overjoyed to see her, embraced her with both arms. She found herself yielding to him and even liking the attention she was getting. Steven, witnessing her whole show, decided enough was enough, storming out of the gallery without looking back. *If Laura thought I would be a push over, she would have another thing coming,* he fumed to himself.

Laura had made her decision and was being carried along with it all. She would deal with Steven tomorrow and try to talk him around. Or so she thought... Having hailed a taxi, he was on his way home to change his life forever. He wanted Laura out of it; all the talk in the world wouldn't make him change his mind. He had witnessed his girlfriend, whom he thought loved him, falling into the arms of another man, and he wasn't going to be made a fool of, not now or ever again.

Chapter 5

Anna and Joseph lived in apartment number two. Lighting candles in their stylish but quaint apartment, they had known the power cut was coming and had been prepared. Setting up her little cherished table in the foyer, always thinking of others, Anna set a battery-operated flickering light so her friends could see when they got home. She laid a bundle of candles on the table, added some matchboxes and went back inside to see to Joseph and his coffee.

Joseph was a tailor, and Anna, a seamstress. They had come to England from Poland in 1970, a newly married twenty-two-year-old Jewish couple, and had somehow managed to build an empire on hard work and determination, never thinking that they would go on to run one of the largest tailoring businesses in England.

Rosenberg's was their legacy. Against all the odds, they had conquered the language barrier, changes in traditions and the way of life. Anna, the stoic mother of two boys, who still found time to sew daily to help in her husband's little corner shop, as he called it, along with Joseph, who could cut a bolt of cloth to fit any shape of man and make him feel like a king, were a formidable team. They grew in stature, loved life, family and their home and as they grew, so too did their workforce, allowing them to forge friendships that would last a lifetime.

Nowadays, they made suits for the gentry of London and supplied well-renowned stores all over the country. Their ever-expanding empire gave a nurturing and loving home to over three hundred tailors and seamstresses alone, with their support staff reaching the five hundred mark by the time they both decided to hand the reins over to their beloved sons, Luther and Isaac, and go into semi-retirement.

Joseph knew he wouldn't be able to walk away fully, deciding to keep a seat on the board and his finger on the pulse of what had become his life's goal. Always knowing the boys were more than capable of taking the business forward into a technological world that he and Anna both knew they weren't part of.

Chapter 6

Telford Parade was in darkness when Steven finally pulled up. He lived above Anna and Joseph, and there were no lights on in his windows or anyone else's. That was unusual as the Rosenbergs were always at home, and their flat was always lit up. They lived in apartment number two, and although an older couple, they were loved by all the tenants as they were good neighbours and very friendly.

Steven entered the lobby and immediately felt that something was not right. Everywhere was in darkness, and the lift was out of order. He went back into the street to see if the lights were off outside; the street, too, was in darkness. He hadn't even noticed this when he pulled up. *A power cut is all I need on a night like tonight*, he thought to himself.

Anna appeared at her door and called out to Steven, "There are candles on the table if you need them, Joseph got some out this morning as the radio said we might have a power cut."

"That would be great," Steven said. How kind they were to everyone. He would thank them properly tomorrow when he popped around for a coffee and a chat, as he usually did.

After lighting his candle and securing a few more in his coat pocket for when he got inside, he bid Anna farewell and headed up the stairs towards his front door to check out if the power cut had caused any damage indoors. Laura would have to wait until he got all of this in order. Clearing out the fridge that had been turned off for hours, he cut some cheese and added a few biscuits. He was hungry; the small snacks offered at the gallery were not enough to keep him going. Thinking hard about his next move, he knew what he wanted to do, and packing her cases wouldn't take him that long.

After all, the flat was his. Laura moved in with him, so many of the possessions inside belonged to him. The few pictures she had bought and the Indian rug she so lovingly chose on their last holiday were packed neatly into a case. He searched the CD pile for all the titles that belonged to her. He would be glad to see the back of some of her music; they really did have such different tastes.

Her clothes and shoes all fitted into a couple of cases, and there was only the bathroom to sort. Laura had every lotion and potion known to man: anti-wrinkle, anti-cellulite, cover this and colour that. Was any of this woman he thought he loved actually real? Her makeup was next; she loved Chanel and bought new products every month. *Wow, she could open her own shop,* Steven thought as he slung the lot into a carrier bag.

Laura would be mortified, but who cared? He was enjoying this and was not going to stop until all traces of her were gone.

Gathering all her belongings together, he opened the front door and placed the bags in the hallway. He knew that if Laura came home really late, she would find all her things, and with the chain on the door, would not be able to get into the flat. Knowing Laura the way he did, he knew that she wouldn't make a fuss and would just leave. She hated a scene that wasn't created for her.

Closing the door, he turned the key in the deadlock, put the chain in place and switched the hall light off. Going into the lounge, he poured himself a very large whisky, lit a cigar and settled in his favourite chair to watch the late-night news before retiring to bed. That big bed would be empty without her, but Steven knew that she would never be a part of his life again, and was sure he could get used to being alone.

Chapter 7

Suzie gazed out of the taxi window as she reached the Mansion House and could see no lights on in the building. *It's a bit early for everyone to be sleeping,* she thought to herself, *something must be wrong.* The power cut was still not sorted, and there were now workmen outside the building; their head torches flickering across the front doors as they went to and fro, trying to figure out the maze of wires that had probably been there since the turn of the last century.

As Suzie let herself into the lobby just by the lift, she could see a small table, set up by Anna, she was sure. On it were some candles, matches and a little flickering light, just giving out enough to see the lobby in its full glory. The wrought iron work on the lift, its concertina gate closed now waiting for the next passenger to pull it open to allow the beauty inside to pour out, for it was a sight to behold. Designed in the 1930s, its Art Deco simplicity making you think of bygone years and romantic times.

The walk up to the next floor was an easy journey, but she loved to take the lift and imagine all the different people that had gone before her. The third-floor button, not used any more as it was now heavily under construction. It was being renovated for a family; new neighbours beckoned. They would fill the top floor, for it was being knocked into one large apartment, the size of which Suzie could only dream. At over four thousand square feet, it would shine like a beacon on top of this majestic block for all to see. Oh, how Suzie loved to imagine what the inside would be like. The only apartment that the lift would stop inside, the buttons fixed with a code that only the select few will have the pleasure to use.

Just as she was taking a candle and lighting it, she heard the apartment door of number one being opened. Standing in nothing but a pair of light grey bottoms was Greg Samuels, her drinks companion from earlier in the day when life seemed rosier and she could take the time to dream.

"Hello there," he said, "I just wanted to make sure you got in all right. I saw you from the window; writers never sleep," he said as he ran his hand through a mass of ebony curls that crowned his head so softly, his hair tousled and pulled, making him look even more handsome than before.

His hazel eyes burrowed into hers, and she had the sudden feeling that she wanted to touch his face, wrap her arms around his chest and feel safe. She snapped out of her thoughts as Greg was speaking, she had not heard a word he had said; dreaming really can wait.

"Your evening, how was it?" he said with a smirk. Her knees were weak beneath her, and she had to steady herself with a hand on the small but exquisite table that she had seen so many times in Anna's beautiful apartment.

"Can I help?" said Greg as he stepped across the lobby, and cradling her elbow into his strong body, he took her into his arms. He smelled of something so familiar and so scrumptious, what was it? "Don't tell me, too much booze and not enough food?" he said with a boyish grin on that oh-so-gorgeous face.

"No, actually I haven't had a drink since lunchtime," Suzie said, feeling as if he were scolding her somehow. "It's probably hunger as I've not had any dinner and I was stood up by my useless husband if you must know!" Cake, he smelled of cake, deep sensual chocolate cake the smell was overpowering. Was she mad, her hunger was making her delirious?

With that, Greg tightened his grip, turned Suzie around and led her into his apartment, before sitting her down at his kitchen table.

He removed her coat and just said in a matter-of-fact voice, "Relax."

There was that smell, dark chocolate lay on the table, broken into tiny pieces, slithers of blackness dark as night ready to be sprinkled over what looked like a plate full of muffins. What was this? He was baking cakes!

"Want one? I just made them before the power went off. it helps me to think when I have a block. Only problem is, I am the only one here to eat them!" he laughed out loud to hide his embarrassment, but Suzie just thought that was adorable. Standing there in just his bottoms, his kitchen table awash with the paraphernalia of baking, she smiled inwardly and helped herself, sprinkling the shards of chocolate across the top for effect.

This man was fast becoming an interesting adventure. Suzie knew this was going to be fun. *Let's hope my waistline can take it*, she thought to herself as she took a bite of what was her first experience of Greg's sensual and amazing cooking skills.

Recipe One — Chocolate Shard Cupcakes (Kim Valentine's Great Grandmother)

250g of self-raising flour
25g cocoa powder
2 teaspoons of baking powder
175g of soft butter
175g of caster sugar
175g of dark chocolate shards, plus 30g for sprinkling
2 large eggs (beaten)
1 teaspoon of vanilla essence
Preheat the oven to 170 degrees centigrade (160 if fan)

Method:

This is an all-in-one method where all ingredients are added together and combined. Once combined whisk on the highest speed for 3 minutes until there are no lumps and the mixture is smooth.

Pour evenly into cupcake cases.

Bake for 20–25 minutes until they are well-risen and spring back when pressed. A cocktail stick should come out clean when inserted.

Leave to cool for a few minutes, before they are totally cool sprinkle the remaining shards of dark chocolate over the top. Share with a loved one!

Chapter 8

"Anna," called Joseph. "Quick, come and see. There he goes, the man from the top floor." Joseph was desperate to meet the elusive Mr Collier but as yet had only seen him fleetingly through the window. "He always seems in such a hurry," he said to his wife as he took her hand to lead her back into their splendid kitchen.

It was the heart of their home, a pot of coffee always simmering on the stove. Anna never gave up her precious coffee pot that belonged to her mother for a modern monstrosity, as she called them.

"It would never make good coffee, and anyway it feels as if Mama is here with me when I start it to boil on the stove," she would tell him. "When the aroma wafts out, I can remember such happy times we had as children, watching Mama make Papa's coffee, listening to their day unfold as we prepared for bed every night. Such happy times, Joseph, my love.

As Joseph poured the coffee, one for his Anna and one for him, hers a special bone china cup that was translucent in the light and his, a mug with 'I love Dad' on the front, long since losing its handle but loved so much it never got thrown away.

They sat in a silence that they both knew so well. After all, who needed constant chit-chat when you loved someone? Words were not needed. Joseph stretched out his hand and lovingly stroked his wife's hair out of her eyes, those big blue eyes that he loved to get lost in. Such memories they both shared of loss, love, accomplishment and now fulfilment. All the money in the world could not bring this happiness that they both felt after forty-five years of marriage.

Luther and Isaac were grown. Anna had wanted a girl, but they were blessed with boys. Joseph often wondered if a girl would have made Anna happier, but she loved her boys and she doted on them both, as much as she did her Joseph. She never forgot him or left him out. They lived in a world that was theirs and theirs alone. Friends were invited in, but as a family, they were strong and secure.

What would the future hold for their two boys, now grown men with families of their own? Luther married to a lovely girl called Ada, and Isaac to Lizzie. Such good boys to their mother and their wives. Three children for Luther, Marjorie his eldest was proving to be somewhat of a whiz in the kitchen even at the age of thirteen. While Maud loved nothing more than watching her father pin and cut fabric. She would sit for hours on his large cutting table, handing him the pins and giggling when he pretended to put them in the wrong place. Albert, their cherished boy, still a toddler, crashed and banged around their family home, always with a toy car in his hand.

Isaac and Lizzie still waiting, hoping and praying for their own little family.

"God is good," his mother was always saying, "Your turn will come."

As they heard the key in the door, their thoughts came back to the here and now.

In burst Isaac yelling "Mum, Dad!"

He had been running; tears streaming down his face, not from sadness, just the cold air making his eyes stream as he ran.

"Oh, Mum, what are we to do? Lizzie is so sick she can't keep anything down and she feels utterly dreadful. I need to work, she needs looking after. Mum, can she come here for a few days? Just until she is better?"

"Shush, shush," soothed Anna as she sat her youngest son down and put a steaming cup of coffee in front of him. "Of course, she can, silly boy. Why didn't you call and bring her? Your Dad will go and pick her up when you have had your coffee. You'll see, everything will be all right."

The apartment was a hive of activity by the time Joseph had driven the four streets to where Isaac and Lizzie now lived. Anna had changed the bed for them, even though nobody had slept in it since they last visited. Always the mother, always thinking of others, she put some pink carnations in a little vase and some old magazines, which she had meant to give to her friend Lucy, beside the bed. Some warm soup was cooking on the stove, and as Lizzie walked in, she wrapped her arms around Anna's neck and hugged her so tight she thought she would break.

"Thank you, Mama, for having me. Isaac is so busy, and I feel so awful. Work has said to stay at home until I feel better." With that, she ran to the bathroom, and Anna could hear the retching from the kitchen. *This is going to be a long few days,* Anna thought as a sudden smile crept across her face. Could it be Lizzie is pregnant?

Chapter 9

The work on the top floor was taking shape. Bobby Collier, his hard hat bright yellow like the sun, was striding through the newly plastered rooms, surveying the sheer magnitude of what would be his final family home.

Well accomplished, distinguished, rich, generous and empathetic — these were just a few of the musings of the journalists that had written about him and his career, which had now spanned over thirty-five years in the construction industry.

As he stopped to take yet another photograph of his beloved home, he couldn't help but think back to the days when it all began. That tiny little apartment on Brixton Hill would be the place where he fell in love with his girl, proposed to her, made love to her and promised to keep her safe forever. Where did all those years go, and why had he got it all so horribly wrong? But more to the point, how did she still love him?

"Mr Collier," a voice behind him broke the silence, and Bobby was back on task, ready to answer any questions they had for him. "This floor, are we tiling or carpeting?"

"Neither," he said with an air of disbelief. Do these people know nothing? "It will be oak throughout, natural, warm and distinctly opulent in its appearance." After all, appearances were everything to Bobby. His life was built on appearances, making sure that everyone only saw what he needed them to see.

The womanising, drinking, gambling and such were all done behind closed doors and in another world, far removed from his beloved sweetheart, Isabella. Sweet, loyal Isabella, as far as he knew. Courageous, honest and a wonderful mother to their four children: Amy, Lilly, Harry and Ava. They all have their mother's eyes and her strong determination. For that, Bobby would always count his blessings.

As he took a last loving glance around his new home, he stepped out onto the landing and took to the stairs, his route for now out of this wonderful building and into the bright sunshine of another new day.

Chapter 10

"Five minutes, Miss Simmonds!" Laura could hardly believe it; she was sitting in her dressing room, waiting to go onto the set of a new drama series for ITV. "Josie's Law," as it was called, was set to be the next best thing on TV, and she had landed the main role, a feisty lady cop with both sex appeal and an ability to fight crime.

Of course, she had to leave Steven behind to do this, but that didn't matter. She had already trodden down one young man in her past, and she was on her way up, and didn't care how she got there or who she hurt on the way. Nick Cole thought that he loved her back in school and then in college, but she wanted bigger and better things in her life. She would show them all; she would succeed without them. Her new name, Lauryl Simmonds, sounded much more like a successful actress, and she was determined to never have to be Laura Nelson again.

David Summers had done what he said he would and got her a big break into TV. She had to be seen with him, and she was invited to so many parties they all just rolled into one. Life for Laura had changed beyond her wildest imagination; Steven Sandgate was a distant memory for her. He would have held her back, caused her to slow down and be cautious. Who needed caution when David Summers was in your corner, spurring you on? Who cared if she had to flirt with him?

"Time to go, Miss Simmonds," Xander said as he popped his head around her dressing room door. Laura, getting to her feet, smoothed down the tiny creases in her jacket. Dressed sexily in a black silk trouser suit, her auburn hair framing her face, the green of her sheer blouse complimenting her eyes, She exuded sex appeal from head to foot. That's what the producers wanted, and that's what they were going to get. Taking a final glance into the mirror, she fixed her hair one last time, and as she strode out into the corridor, she pushed all thoughts of Steven out of her head. She didn't need him; she was on her way, and nobody was going to take this moment away from her.

Laura was glad to hear the final message from the director, "Time to go home!"

Dying to take off the four-inch patent black shoes that seemed to be welded to her feet. *Who knew TV could be this hard and warrant such concentration?* she thought to herself. If every day was going to be like this, she needed to gain some stamina, and she knew exactly who could help her.

As she picked up her phone, she began to dial his number without even thinking. It went straight to answerphone so, without hesitation, she spoke in that unforgettable sexy tone that he knew so well.

"Nick, it's me, Lauryl, Laura," she corrected herself. "I need your help, please call me back when you have time. It's very important." As she hung up the phone, she wondered if he would call back. Had he forgiven her for setting him up on that blind date with her friend Katie? Turned out that Katie was a bit of a control freak and pushed poor Nick to the edge and back again. He was never allowed out, not without her; she was convinced that he was in love with Laura. But they were just good friends, he knew that, didn't he? Surely, he had forgiven her by now?

It had been two years since she had seen him, and she knew he was the only one that could help — the only one who really knew her. He was her friend from way back, when life was easier and their childhood dreams were connected to each other. He was her first friend; he was always there, no matter what! Now an independent fitness instructor with clients from all walks of life, a TV deal on a morning show and his own brand of fitness wear. Would he want to go down that route again of helping her?

As she eased herself into a warm bath filled with the glorious scents of lavender, her thoughts drifted back to Nick — his mousey brown hair and large dark brown eyes that would stare right into her inner being. His toned body stood at five feet nine inches, but every bit of him was refined and honed into a perfect specimen of health and fitness. His brand of fitness wear, with its tell-tale logo, flashed into her head. What did the "L" stand for in N&L Fitness? He never did tell her. As she dreamt of old times, her eyes closed, the bubbles popping around her, she could hear her phone in the distance, and she knew the familiar ringtone from their past — Nick was calling back!

Chapter 11

The alarm went off at 5 a.m. and Suzie woke with a start. Where was Max? She couldn't feel him in the bed beside her. As she moved her arm across the beautiful Egyptian linen that she loved so much, it felt cold to her touch and made her scoot her hand back into the warmth of her side of the bed.

He hadn't come home again last night. This was becoming a regular occurrence since he stood her up at the art gallery. *Not more surgeries out of the blue,* she thought to herself. That excuse was getting a little old now.

After what seemed like the quickest shower and change in history, dressed in casual jeans and a beautiful sheer blouse, Suzie slipped her feet into her beloved Gabor loafers picked up her Hermes bag and closed the front door behind her. There wasn't a sound to be heard in the block. Was Greg awake? Did he know how much of an effect he had on her? So many questions and no time to find out.

The car drew up outside as she stepped out of the lobby door, a beautiful black Bentley, dark and sleek like a panther. She slid herself into the back seat, its luxurious grey leather wrapping around her like a safety blanket. One final glance back at the block. Greg was there, stretching his torso in full view, his ebony hair curled against his forehead, and his big hazel eyes smiling as they found hers. A vision that would last all day. She knew without a shadow of a doubt that she had to see him again.

She waved a final farewell and smiled inwardly. He did think of her, and he had remembered that she was leaving for a meeting in Cambridge, a meeting that could change the face of Crichton's forever. They had met for coffee many times, loving the fact that they could tell each other anything. Suzie felt comfortable with Greg, and they relaxed into each other whenever they met.

The car sped through the city centre and headed to the motorway. Her driver told her that the M11 was busy as usual and her trip to Cambridge would take a few hours.

Suzie stretched out and kicked her loafers off. She loved those shoes. They were like faithful companions, bought from a little boutique in Greenwich where she liked to shop for bargains and little forgotten treasures for the apartment. Her feet felt the luxury of the fitted carpet, and she poured herself a sparkling water. After all, they had sent this beautiful car for her; she may as well make the most of it. Her little red Golf GTi, carefully stored in the underground car park below the Mansion block, would never have been good enough to park outside the offices of Jordan & Cleeve, one of the most prestigious fashion houses in the United Kingdom.

Her hopes and dreams were going to be put to the test today. Could she really be going to sign the biggest deal in Crichton's history? Mary Cleeve, who had called her personally to invite her, had made all the right noises and was very excited to meet Suzie. Jordan was the one that would be a hard nut to crack. Would he see that this young lady, 'just a slip of a girl,' as he had called her, could and would be a force to be reckoned with in years to come?

The car was travelling steadily through the busy traffic, slicing its way now like a knife through butter. The skyline visibly pushing forward the enormity of the Jordan & Cleeve building.

"A blot on the landscape," some have said, but to Suzie, it was a sight to behold. Its glass facade shimmered like an evening gown at the Oscars. The time had come to show the rest of the design world just what Suzie Crichton was made of.

Chapter 12

He could see her coming from his second-floor window; there was no mistaking the striking features. Her hair had grown, with small flyaway curls jutting out under her brown beret, jauntily placed to show off the bright green of her eyes. The sun had kissed her face, giving off a radiant glow. He remembered all too well the effect she had on him. Knowing he had to be strong, she had hurt him in the past. One smile from Laura and he was putty in her hands. He had to get this over and done with and get her out of his life forever. He had a future that was far more important than a mere infatuation with an old flame.

Remembering back to that night, he didn't know when it had happened, but in the morning the bags were gone, and there was no sign of Laura. Had she come back in the middle of the night and not been able to get in, or had she come back the next morning and discovered her bags? He would never know, and he had hoped that she wouldn't contact him in any way. Being hurt like that was never going to happen to him again; he would make sure of that.

He had decided not to go to work the next day and phoned in sick. He knew that he didn't sound sick and wondered if his boss knew he was lying. He didn't really care; he was going to be alone for the first time in over two years, and he had to get it straight in his head before he could tackle other people and the pleasantries of life in a busy office.

Steven was a lawyer and loved nothing more than standing in court defending his clients. He was all out of talk at the moment, and a few days off was all he needed. He had to exorcise Laura from his life, and he had decided a haircut and some new clothes would go a long way to helping him.

Oxford Street was packed, and Steven soon realised that he hated shopping. Laura had always gone with him and given him her opinion on his clothes. Did he even know what suited him? He had relied on other people for so long that he had forgotten what it was like, and this was something that he was going to have to change? A new Steven and a new life lay ahead.

Now today, Laura was at the door. As she stepped into the apartment, the air was filled with the oh-so-familiar scent of Coco Chanel, a far cry from the more comforting aroma of Miss Dior that Jessica so effortlessly wore.

He had bought the Chanel for their first Valentine's Day. They had been dating for a while, and she had protested that he didn't need to buy her a present, but he couldn't turn up at the restaurant empty-handed. The assistant in the shop had told him it was the best one to buy. *She must know,* he thought to himself. Matched with a yellow rose and the smallest card he could find, after all, he didn't want to overwhelm her, he was all set. The memory of that day was as sharp in his mind as if it were yesterday.

Laura waltzed passed him, threw off her shiny black Christian Louboutin shoes, their classic red soles catching the light overhead, and perched herself on the sofa. Its leather creaked and moaned as if it remembered her last visit.

"A coffee would be nice darling," she drawled, as if she were still on the set of her fabulous new drama; isn't that what the critics had called it?

"What do you want?" Steven asked with an air of discomfort. How dare she think she could sidle back in here after six months without a goodbye. Not a word from her since he left all her belongings out in the hall on that fateful night. He felt betrayed, and he wasn't going to let her worm her way back into his life. He had moved on and was enjoying being in a real relationship.

"Oh darling, don't be like that. I just need a tiny favour. I need an escort for the night of the twenty-third and thought you would be the perfect fit. People have seen us together before, so there won't be any photographers wanting to know who the new man in my life is! Marvellous idea don't you think?"

"No, I don't think. What right have you got to swan back in here after all you have done and said about me?

I do read the tabloids, you know. Assuming that I would just fall at your feet and do as you ask. I have more respect for myself than that, and I thought you would have at least had a little for me too. You hurt me more than words could say, humiliating me in front of our friends, and you expect me to roll over and play nicely.

"Get your shoes, pick up your belongings and get out of my life. You deserve all you get, Laura Nelson. Oh no, that's not your name any more, is it? Lauryl Simmonds, I forgot you changed your identity because Laura Nelson just sounded way too boring, isn't that what you said in Hello! last month?"

With that, Steven opened the front door for the very last time, and Laura Nelson walked out of his life forever. He was happier than he had been in years. Jessica would be around later on, and he didn't want anything to ruin what he hoped would be the best decision he had made in his life.

Chapter 13

"Suzie, how lovely to see you," Mary Cleeve dressed in her tell-tale black shift dress and patent sling-backs held out her hand. Suzie could feel the delicate, paper-like skin as she very gently but firmly took it into hers. Trying to decide whether to hug or not, in the end, Mary grabbed hold of her and hugged her so tightly that Suzie thought she would die.

Mary Cleeve had created a range of workwear for ladies of a certain age and insisted on wearing it herself to work, to ensure it never felt dated or old. She carried it off with faultless ease; her size ten frame and at five feet ten inches, she fitted beautifully like a dressmaker's dummy into the sheer silk fabric. Its cut was superb, and every nip and tuck was sewn delicately by her seamstresses, their attention to detail showing in her every move.

"Come, come," she ushered Suzie into the great sprawling conference room. It was situated on the thirty-second floor of the Jordan & Cleeve building, so modern it made Suzie's head turn. The light poured in through the sheet glass windows, their floor-to-ceiling expanse capturing every facet of the skyline outside.

Suzie found herself feeling a little giddy; her fear of heights never allowed her too near the edge of any building so she would truly never see what the windows had in store.

Settling herself in one of the thirty or so chairs encircling the vast jarrah wood table, Suzie could feel her heart pounding. Mary Cleeve was offering her the chance of a lifetime, and even her husband Jordan had come on board after much wrangling and cajoling. All Suzie had to do now was sign on the dotted line, and her business would be in partnership with the largest clothing distributors in London, Paris and New York.

The Jordan & Cleeve brand was known worldwide, and their clothing was worn by all walks of life. They had managed many years ago to offer clothing to both satisfy the couture need and the off the peg ranges. The likes of Harvey Nichols, Selfridges, John Lewis and now even New Look carried their brand and carried it well.

Mary Cleeve had been a tour de force when, as a young fashion designer in the '60s, her mini skirts and A-lines were a contrasting hit among her clients, and they loved her diversity.

When she met Jordan, he was a struggling chef, and he wanted more in his life than long gruelling hours and poor pay. At six feet two inches, he complimented her completely, his long flowing hair and an impeccable dress sense for a man at that time. She loved how he wore a suit, always contrasting his tie and his socks to add that little dash of colour and flair. He knew how men wanted to dress, and as time went on, he offered her a taste of the unknown, the eye of the man on the street. With long hours and study, Jordan soon became the head of his own emporium, a force to be reckoned with, and a brand name in every store across the United Kingdom.

After their marriage in the late '70s, they joined forces and the Jordan & Cleeve brand took on a new face, in a new city, and eventually across the world.

"Just sign here, Miss Crichton, where you see the crosses and date, please." The lawyer flicked effortlessly through the pages, picking out every page that had a little pink-coloured tag on it. "Your lawyer has agreed every part of the contract, and it's just up to you now."

As Suzie signed her delicate name onto every page, her Mont Blanc pen gliding effortlessly across the smooth, silky pages. She couldn't help but smile to herself. This was what she had been working so hard on for the last two years. The extra hours, the planning, the designs and the sleepless nights were all culminating here. This was the last link in the chain; once she had signed everything, there was no going back. Crichton's and the Jordan & Cleeve brand would be in a collaborative partnership to bring more fashion ideas to the high streets of many cities across the world. 2014 was looking to be a great year. Their plans to conquer not only the rest of Europe but more of America and beyond were set in stone and ready to roll. Suzie Crichton had arrived, and she had done it with the help of her team and her sheer determination.

Chapter 14

Dressed impeccably, the blue Boss suit fitting where it touched, his lean body being caressed by the exquisite fabric. His crisp white shirt was a testament to his need for a professional look that screamed good taste, and his tie was a vibrant orange to match his socks. Suzie had bought them on their last visit to Covent Garden; she insisted he had them after reading an article on Jordan & Cleeve in Vogue: "Five Top Tips for the Well-Dressed Man," its tagline. All the while, Suzie just thought it would make his white shirts a little less boring.

Max strode across the concourse of the building with ease. He knew every raised paving slab, the colour of the tiles telling a story as he stepped with purpose towards his office. As he opened the door to his contemporary space, its light shades of blue and teal usually a calming influence; he could feel the pressure of the night before searing through his veins. What would he say to Suzie? How could he explain? He looked at his phone: six missed calls and a text message that just said, Where are you?. How could he have slipped up again and not gone home? His flat, a little one-bedroomed apartment in the heart of London was a stone's throw from the tube. He could easily have gone back; why hadn't he?

Suzie was so preoccupied with Crichton's she hardly noticed him these days. The constant meetings, phone calls and planning meant that he got pushed further and further down the pecking order. Did she not realise that he was getting restless? He needed more than she could offer, and he was oh so tired of the conversations about having a family. It wasn't on his grand plan, and he wasn't changing that for anyone; not even Suzie.

His large white chair was a welcome blessing. His whole body ached from the night before, his muscles remembering every move that he and Holly, his assistant, had made.

Holly was twenty-three and quite stunning, nothing like Suzie at all, really. She was five feet ten and athletic, her heels she wore to the office accentuating her calf muscles and the tone of her long, sleek legs. Her skirts were deliberately above her knees to show off how toned and tanned she was. She loved the tanning salon and made every effort to remain sun-kissed and toned at all times. Her trips to the gym every other day clearly defining her whole body. She wanted Max right from the start, and she was going to have him. He knew that the first time he had met her; she told him he was going to be hers. Max had laughed it off and clearly stated that he was happily married. Holly had roared with laughter, her long blonde hair cascading across her face as she tilted her head back and forth as she laughed.

"Oh, Max, there is no such thing as a happily married man; you have no idea what happy really means," she laughed.

This was eleven months ago; within two weeks, Holly was a permanent fixture at Max's flat. He kept this place on in case they needed it. That's what he told Suzie. As far as she was concerned, it had been shut up for over two years and was just there as a safety net.

Max turned with a start as his office door swung open and Holly came in, her ice-blue eyes giving nothing away about the night before, her blonde hair tumbling across her shoulders, making Max want to run his fingers through it. Business as usual, they went through his appointments, his operations and his diary for the coming week. All the while, Holly kept her distance from Max. At work, she was all professional and never got too close. She wanted Max to want her, and want her he did.

As she sat across from him, she could see him looking at her intently, noticing the cut of her suit, how she contrasted her accessories and how she wore it well. A small smile spread across his face. What was he doing? He was thinking about Suzie, How would she wear this suit? What would she put with it? Holly looked on, assuming he was smiling at her. She was pulling him in deeper and deeper. Max was torn between the safety of home and the thrill of Holly.

Chapter 15

"Where on earth have you been?" Suzie shouted at Max as she heard him throw his keys onto the hall stand, a habit he had been doing since they bought the aged oak piece whilst out antiquing in the heart of the Kent countryside one day. Tenterden was their favourite place to 'mooch', as they both called it. Arm in arm sauntering around the plethora of antique shops and bric-a-brac stalls strewn across the pavements and grassy areas.

"Suzie, you are not going to believe this, but I got called into a surgery just as I was leaving the building last night, and my phone died. It was so late to come home that I stayed in the flat. It was so dusty I had to shake out all the bedding before I could get in." All the time his smile was fixed on her, his steely grey eyes piercing through her, willing her to believe him.

"Oh, darling, that's just too bad," she found herself saying. She didn't care whether she believed him or not. Today had been her day, the day that begins the rest of her life. She had signed one of the most lucrative deals in the history of her company, and times were changing.

Tomorrow, she thought to herself, tomorrow I will tackle the truth, not today.

"Champagne?" Max said, "What are we celebrating?" As Suzie walked towards him, the exquisite Villeroy and Boch glasses overflowing with the effervescence of excitement, the bubbles all jostling each other, fighting for the top of the glass.

She rested a glass gently into his hand and just said matter-of-factly, "Crichton's is now officially in business with the Jordan & Cleeve Company. We signed the deal today, and my little company is on the up. I didn't want to tell you yet because nothing had been finalised."

Suzie's excitement was so apparent that Max didn't have the heart to chastise her. Why hadn't she told him about it before? He could have helped, he would have helped, wouldn't he? But no, this discussion could wait for another day. He was reprieved by the skin of his teeth, and this news was taking the heat off him.

The evening ended where it always did after too much champagne and very little food. Suzie never could drink more than three glasses of bubbles; it made her sleep. As they headed towards their bedroom, thoughts of Holly and Greg in their minds, their clothes discarded as they headed to the bed. Suzie knew that he would be cross; he hated not having sex, and after all, he had said it was his right as a husband. But as they lay, there the silence was broken by the low murmurings of breath. Suzie was blissfully sleeping, and Max wanted Holly.

Chapter 16

Nick knew that this was his one and only chance to repay Laura, Lauryl, whatever her name was now, for what she had put him through. Katie was an absolute control freak and nutter — that's what his friends had called her. She was that and so much more, and above all else, it really was the last straw.

Katie had been one of Laura's friends, and she had suggested they go out as she had decided that she didn't want him in her life any longer.

He was never allowed out, not without Katie, and if he mentioned Laura, it was as if he had poured vinegar on a wound. She physically lashed out and accused him of being unfaithful; saying that she would never let him be alone with Laura ever again.

She had stalked him on social media and befriended all his friends, making comments on posts that he shared and making it all seem as if everything in their world were rosy. If Laura thought she was going to get away with that scot-free, well, she could think again!

The years he had wasted on that girl, loving her and wanting her. He even named his company after her —

N&L Fitness was his brand. Did she not know that Nick and L fitness was a tribute to her?

He knew that she could be selfish; she was beautiful, and men had flocked to her like moths to a flame. Her auburn hair made her stand out, making every woman around pale into insignificance once she smiled through those beautiful green eyes. Why had he let himself love her for so many years?

He had called her back a few nights before when she had left a message saying she needed his help. After all this time, she decides to make contact. All that wasted time, making sure she had everything that she needed as a teenager. Making sure she had her lunch at school and carrying her bags from class to class. She let him follow her around like a lost puppy for all that time.

Then, at college, they had gone to the same one, as he did sport and she did performance for film and television. Meeting every break time to buy her drinks and food, she was always saying she had no money, and Nick, being Nick, had put his hand in his pocket and paid for everything. Never really knowing if their relationship was ever going to go further than him being totally in love with her and Laura just taking what she could. His friends said that he was mad, that she was using him, but he wouldn't listen, and he hoped above everything that she would one day feel for him what he did for her. Did she not know that he was totally in love with her?

"What does she want with me?" he found himself saying out loud. He had no idea, but he had loved her for long enough; it was time.

Chapter 17

Steven found himself wandering around the apartment, plumping up the cushions, straightening the photograph frames on Granny's chest and switching on the lamps that he had positioned to allow for a sense of opulence and romantic lighting. Jessica looked the picture of loveliness in her coral dress and matching bag. She was such a far cry from the high maintenance of his past girlfriends, and he wanted everything to be perfect for her, making sure everything was just so for the evening. After all, it wasn't every night that a man proposed.

"Where on earth are we going tonight?" Jessica asked as Steven led her into the sitting room; she did love his apartment. The vibrant colours of his bachelor pad, his attention to detail and his ability to match everything so effortlessly. Steven had such lovely pieces of furniture; he had told her that the cocktail cabinet was once his mother's, and she had sewn a wedding dress to buy it. A treasured piece that he said he would never want to lose. The beautiful mahogany chest that once belonged to his great-grandmother was adorned with exquisite glass frames of all shapes and sizes. She smiled as she noticed he had put a picture of them when they went to the theatre in one of the large ornate frames. She could see herself smiling up into his dark blue eyes, his lovely blond hair cascading over his forehead as he leant down to kiss her gently on her nose. That feeling when he kissed her made her tummy go into knots, and she felt like a teenage girl in love.

Steven entwined his arm around her waist and spun her around.

"Hello, beautiful lady," he said as he kissed her ever so gently at first, then with more passion. "I will tell you when we get there," he said, smiling all the time.

"Oh, you spoilsport," Jessica squealed as he tickled her ribs and made her squirm.

Jessica was a lawyer in the same firm as Steven. It was usually frowned upon to date one's colleagues, but everyone said they were a perfect fit; they seemed to encourage the union rather than admonish it. She was a divorce lawyer, *of course she was,* he thought to himself. Jessica was the kindest, most empathetic person he had ever met, and she went the extra mile for everyone that she came into contact with.

Jessica would say she was just doing her job, but Steven knew that this was much more than a job to her; it was a vocation. He admired her determination and guts when faced with difficult decisions and cases and he hoped that one day she would share with him some of the difficult information that she had to deal with on a daily basis. If not just to pry, but so that he could ease some of the pressure that she was undoubtedly under and allow him to soothe her when she needed help.

"Come on then," he said as he held up her coat for her. Jessica loved that he was always the gentleman and putting her first. Such an endearing quality in a man.

"Ooh can we go in the lift?" she smiled as she spoke. Jessica loved the lift as much as she loved Steven. The realisation hit her like a proverbial brick; she was in love with Steven. The gated lift came to a halt on the ground floor, and Anna was outside her apartment watering some daisies she had placed in the window box outside her kitchen window.

"Hello, you two. Jessica, you look lovely. Have fun tonight," she winked at Steven as he went past and mouthed without speaking out loud, "good luck."

Steven had been a regular visitor around Anna and Joseph's kitchen table. He had called in a few nights ago to show them the ring he had bought for Jessica. It was very small and understated, a vibrant sapphire set with diamonds. Jessica wasn't into flashy jewellery and loved tasteful pieces.

"It's beautiful!" Anna shrieked when he opened the box. Joseph agreed wholeheartedly, and a toast was made with their coffee cups.

"To you and Jessica!" they both cheered in unison.

The taxi was waiting for them as they stepped outside of the beautifully ornate glass doors. The sliver glistening in the lamp light from above, the beautifully made number pad beside the entrance looking as if it would be best placed on the set of an old black and white film. Oh, how they both loved this building.

"Could you imagine the stories that lift could tell?" Jessica said as she climbed into the waiting car.

The journey didn't take long at all. In fact, Jessica thought they could have walked it easily enough, but she didn't say anything to Steven; this was his surprise, and she wanted to indulge him. After all, it wasn't every day she got whisked away by a handsome man.

As they drove through the streets, she could see the houses nearby all lit up and wondered what all the people inside were up to. Making dinner, watching television, kids quarrelling and Mums berating them. Jessica knew one day that she wanted that life; she longed for that life. To be a wife and mother as well as a lawyer would be a dream come true. She had seen so many marriages at their worst; surely, they couldn't all be that bad, could they?

Looking out of the window, she could see the skyline ahead.

"No!", she cried out. "We are not going there, are we?" Straight ahead was the Oxo Tower, high above all the other buildings around it, its iconic sign lit up in the night sky, a beacon to the boats that would have sailed past it every night.

Steven couldn't contain his delight; his smile from ear to ear made her realise they were, and she stretched her hand out to squeeze his in thanks for remembering.

She had told him once when they first met that it was on her bucket list of places she had always wanted to visit.

Inside, they headed to the bar and ordered a couple of glasses of champagne,

"Why not?" Steven said. "Let's start as we mean to go on." Jessica took the glass from him, and she could feel the bubbles popping on her face as she took her first sip. The excitement in the glass was as effervescent as her own mounting joy at being in this place.

"Your table will be fifteen minutes, Mr Sandgate," the waiter informed them. "Why not enjoy the view while you wait?" As Jessica looked up from her glass, the full London skyline came into view and she was enchanted by its beauty. With so many lights and so much going on, this city really didn't seem to sleep.

Their meal was lovely; they had prepared a special gluten-free menu for Jessica as she had found out a few years before that she was coeliac and had to avoid certain foods. Their choices had been amazing and so very thoughtful of Steven, as eating out was tricky at the best of times.

As they sipped their Cognac at the end of the meal, Jessica could see that Steven was beginning to look a bit uneasy.

"I hope you are okay, darling," she said and then jokingly, "Oh no, you didn't forget your wallet, did you?"

They both laughed, and he said, "Do you not fancy doing the washing up then?"

With that, Steven was up out of his chair like a flash and down on one knee. At first, she thought he was having a heart attack or something. Then she saw the look on his face and realized everything was going to be okay.

"Will you marry me, please, Jessica Edwards, and make me the happiest man alive?"

The sudden rush of relief on his face was apparent, and Jessica had no hesitation at all.

"Oh my goodness, yes, of course I will!" she said with the biggest smile on her face. The waiters were clapping, the other diners were clapping. Steven was up on his feet, pulling her to him, his kiss warm and inviting. Jessica felt as if she were dreaming, had she just said yes to marriage? Oh, my goodness, life could not be any better. Jessica and Steven were getting married.

Chapter 18

Anna busied herself in the kitchen, allowing Lizzie to clean herself up and called out to her, "Get yourself straight into bed, I will be along in a minute."

She couldn't help but wonder, was Lizzie really poorly or was this something else? This was the second time that Lizzie had come to stay, feeling wretched and being sick. It seemed as though it would never stop.

After having two boys of her own, she spotted the tell-tale signs of morning sickness, whoever called it that was surely mistaken. Anna could remember with Isaac she was sick morning, noon and night. She had to be hospitalised in the end; they worried so much about her not nourishing the baby enough and all the loss of fluids. It was a very traumatic time, but they just kept telling her everything would be okay.

Anna closed her eyes and said a little prayer, "Please God make this be what we have hoped and prayed for; Lizzie would be a great Mum." As she strode across the kitchen, a hot cup of tea and some chicken soup in hand, Anna smiled to herself and as gently as possible soothed Lizzie with her words.

"Darling girl," she said. "Everything is going to be just fine; Mama is here and I will look after you."

Lizzie felt dreadful, the nausea kept coming in waves and she couldn't keep anything inside her. Worried that the smell of the chicken soup would make her wretch, she pleaded with Anna to take it away.

Anna propped her up and said with her soft voice, "Come on Lizzie, just a few mouthfuls, it will do you the world of good and we must keep up your strength." Always obliging and not wanting to hurt her feelings, Lizzie did as she was told and remarkably it was very good. What on earth did she put into that soup? It was just warm enough to drink and tasted amazing.

Lizzie felt a smile creep across her face as Anna bent down gently to kiss the top of her head.

"Now go to sleep," she said, "And you will feel so much better for the rest." Lizzie let herself slide further down into the bed and allowed the warmth and cosiness to soothe her. Soon, she was breathing easy and Anna knew that was her cue to leave.

Joseph had poured himself a coffee and was flicking through some papers at the kitchen table.

"Everything is looking good for the boys to take over, Anna, my love," he said, peering over the top of his tiny round glasses that he had been wearing on and off for over twenty years.

Anna leaned in as she went past and kissed him on the cheek, blushing ever so slightly as she always did when she felt the warmth of her beloved Joseph's skin on her lips. Joseph loved that she still wanted to kiss him after all these years; she was his best friend and his soulmate. If anything ever happened to Anna, he knew that he would not be able to live without her.

"Have you told the boys yet?" Anna enquired, knowing full well that he hadn't. They had decided to wait until all the paperwork was finalised before sharing the news with their two sons. They both worked so hard; this would undoubtedly give them more work. But Joseph knew that they both could handle it, and they had a great team of people working alongside them. With Esther and Immanuel, the four of them would undoubtedly succeed.

"Joseph," Anna said in a very quiet voice, almost a whisper, in case Lizzie would wake up and hear her. "Do you think Lizzie might be pregnant?" Joseph took his glasses off, as he always did with his left hand, and ran his fingers through his hair. It was grey now but still as thick as it was when he was a young man and Anna first fell in love with him.

"Honestly, Anna, what a notion. The girl is sick and weary." He placed his glasses back on his face, and Anna knew that was the end of the subject for now. She would keep an eye on Lizzie and see if she could do a little detective work at the same time.

Knowing that she needed to tread carefully where Lizzie was concerned, Isaac was very protective of his young wife, and Joseph, well, he was just Joseph. If it wasn't blatantly obvious, he just ticked along thinking everything was just fine. Busying herself with the chores in hand, making dinner for four now instead of two, and taking care of her beloved family had to be her first priority. Anna had everything she needed right here, and Lizzie would soon be up and about, and she could talk to her then.

As he placed the key in the door, Isaac was taken back to his carefree days of growing up. After all, this was the only home he had ever known before Lizzie. His mum and dad were always supportive, allowing him to make his own decisions. The familiar smells of cooking and coffee wafted from the kitchen, and as he walked in, he smiled to himself that nothing had changed. They were both still there, still the head of the family and taking care of business.

"Hello, Dad," Isaac said as he walked over and patted his dad on the back. They weren't much for hugging, her boys, so this was as near to affection that she could hope from them both. Anna stretched out her arms, and Isaac gave her that knowing look.

"Oh, Mum, I am too old for all that nonsense."

Anna grabbed him anyway and said, "Hug your mother; I might not be here next year." Isaac laughed so loud it woke Lizzie, and he scooped his mum up in his arms and hugged her tightly. "That's better, now go and see you wife," Anna said.

As Isaac walked out into the hallway, he took a last look back at his mum. She was never happier than when her boys came home for a visit. One day he hoped there would be grandkids too.

"Hello, my little peach," he said as he cradled Lizzie in his arms. She looked so small and frail in that big bed, the sleep still in her eyes and her hair all tousled and falling onto her face. She was such a delicate young thing, twenty-three and as small as small could be, compared to his nearly six-foot stature.

He had loved Lizzie from the moment he had seen her in the bookstore where she worked. Her dark hair and eyes drew him in, and he found himself tongue-tied in her presence. *How could she be so beautiful?* he had thought to himself. Would a girl like that even look at a man like me?

Lizzie looked up into his hazel eyes and drank in their darkness. She had been captivated by this handsome tailor. She had seen him in the bookstore before with his friends and had inquired what he did.

"Oh, don't you know, Isaac? He is the heir to the throne," he said jokingly. "He is from the Rosenberg kingdom." She had no idea what he meant; she was just enthralled by this man she hadn't even spoken a word to.

"Hello, darling," she said. "I am feeling a little better tonight, after your mama's chicken soup." Isaac just smiled; he knew what good medicine his mum's chicken soup was, and he knew that Lizzie was in safe hands.

Recipe Two — Chicken Soup & Matzo dumplings (Kim Valentine's Great Grandmother)

1 large whole chicken
8 carrots chopped into small chunks
1 large onion chopped
2 parsnips cored and chopped into small chunks
3 cloves of crushed garlic
2 sticks of celery trimmed and chopped into small chunks
1 bunch of fresh chopped dill
Salt and pepper to season, to taste
For the Matzo balls
330g Matzo meal (ground Matzo crackers)
6 eggs
6 tablespoons of vegetable oil
2 teaspoons of salt

Method:
Breast side down, place your chicken in a large pot and add all of your cut vegetables but not the garlic, fill with water so that it covers everything in the pot. Bring the pot to a simmer (but do not let it boil) and with the lid partially on allow to cook for 2 hours; remember to skim the froth from the pot as it simmers.

After 2 hours skim the fat from the top and then add the cloves of garlic, keeping it partially covered and simmer for a further 2 hours.

In another bowl mix the Matzo ingredients together with 4 tablespoons of the chicken soup broth. Place this mixture in the fridge for approximately 30 minutes.

After the second 2 hours pass the soup through a sieve to remove all the solids, place the broth back into the pot and add the Matzo balls. Allow the soup to boil then bring to a simmer and cover, cooking the balls for 30 minutes.

Take all the meat from the bones and when the balls are cooked add this and the vegetables to the pot. Season to taste and enjoy.

Chapter 19

The party invitations had gone out, and Suzie was getting more excited as the day came closer. She had waited so long for this collaboration between herself and Mary. She wanted everyone to know that this was going to change the face of the business as they knew it.

Mary Cleeve had said, "You do it all, Suzie. Jordan and I will just turn up and join in." She valued Mary's friendship and her complete trust in Suzie to do what was needed.

Her connections in the world of fashion would bring forward many blasts from the past as well as newcomers and potential clients. The invitation list was filled with models, TV personalities, friends, family and everyone Suzie felt should be included in this momentous occasion.

As she put the phone down from chatting over menus with the hotel, her mind wandered to her last encounter with Greg. He had been coming out of his apartment when she was coming home the other day. There hadn't been time to stop and chat, even though she found herself wanting to. Every single day, she wanted to tell Greg this or that and let him know what was happening in her world. She wondered what he was doing, how his novel coming along, and whether he had he made any more cakes. Memories of that evening still fresh in her mind — the sensual chocolate, his warm body catching her and then leading her into his apartment. Suzie made a mental note to go and see him soon. She needed to see him.

The phone rang, and Suzie snatched it up, seeing that it was the venue calling. She had decided on The Great Room in the basement of the Grosvenor House in Park Lane. It once housed an ice-skating rink where the Queen, as a then Princess, learned to skate at the age of seven. Many of the original workings of the rink are still housed beneath the floor. It was a perfect choice, as its sheer beauty could be seen shining through in every crystal chandelier and wine glass that adorned the ceilings and tables when laid for a banquet.

Suzie had opted for a large dance floor and less formal table arrangements, knowing her clientele and their desire to party. The linens had all been chosen in her favourite shades of blue, ranging from sky to turquoise. Each one had been hand-chosen, and they would be displayed exactly as Suzie had imagined it. The florist, Paul Thomas, was from Mayfair and had made many displays for her over the years. Peter, her old friend, just knew exactly what she needed; his attention to detail was impeccable, and the company's personal service was bar none. Suzie was leaving nothing to chance, as the eyes of the world's press would be on her that night, and she needed everything to go without a hitch. Feeling satisfied that she had everything in hand, Suzie decided to take the bull by the horns and see if Greg was up for a coffee and a chat. After all, what harm could that do?

Clutching an invitation to her chest, Suzie took the stairs down to Greg's apartment, her heart racing as the steps brought her closer and closer to the adorable man who had fed her chocolate cake and listened to her woes. His front door, black like everyone's, shone like a newly polished diamond. All painted the same colour, yet each apartment had so many different stories unfolding inside every day.

The knock on the door rendered his characters still, until the next time he would sit down and paint their pictures for his readers to explore. His new glasses were still on top of his head, their gold frames skimming the light as he moved. He was always looking for them, so he took to wearing them like a beloved hat, always there ready and waiting for their next adventure. His novel, now reaching the end, had seen him back and forth many times across the chapters, editing, spelling and correcting grammar; all ready for his editor, Tracy, to proofread and critique.

Greg rarely had visitors during the day; his friends usually called beforehand. They all knew that once he got into a book, he had to focus and just get it done. Turning up unannounced usually saw them turning on their heels and heading back where they came from.

His face was unshaven and drawn, the three-day-old stubble jutting out like little needles from a pincushion. Wearing just a pair of shorts, he opened the door, and to his surprise, there she was. Suzie, the woman who had filled his dreams and thoughts for the last few months. She was standing on his doorstep, the beautiful pale green dress she had chosen accentuating her small frame, bringing out the colour in her eyes. He couldn't help but smile, a smile that said hello, how are you? I wanted to see you and I missed you, all at once.

He pulled a sweater off the coat rack and eased it over his head. His torso tight and muscular; Suzie tried not to stare, her mouth open just a little too far. She sensed his happiness, so she relaxed enough to smile back and thrust out her hand with the invitation in it. As Greg scanned the card, its navy-blue lettering raised beneath his fingers, he opened the door fully and for the first time, Suzie spoke.

"Sorry I haven't been to see you sooner; I have been rushed off my feet." Greg knew this was the case as he had seen her coming and going from his window as he tapped away on his keyboard, ever grateful for her return. Somehow just knowing she was upstairs made him feel closer to her.

"Never mind all that," he said with the biggest smile, "You are here now, and that's all that matters."

As they exchanged stories of this and that, Suzie told him all about the party she was throwing. They both felt comfortable together. Their chattering flowed, and they bounced off each other; each of them giving the other time to speak before telling their own tales. Coffees were drunk, and Greg apologised that there were no cakes as he was writing again and only made them when he had a total block. He knew that since meeting Suzie, his thoughts of romance had awakened, and he found he could write for hours at a time, often missing meals so that he didn't forget to write a single thing down. Suzie, not hiding her disappointment, gave out a little sigh.

"Maybe next time," she said. Her sweet tooth would not be satisfied today, she thought.

The time passed so quickly that neither of them gave it a thought. When Suzie's alarm shrieked, they both jumped. The alien noise had broken the spell and was telling them it was time for Suzie to go. As she gathered her thoughts and picked up her phone, she reached over and kissed Greg very gently on the cheek. His skin was prickly, but smelling of Gaultier, was warm and inviting. She lingered a little too long as she drank in the alluring aroma, finding herself blushing beneath his gaze.

"Thanks for the coffee," she found herself saying as she fumbled for the lock on the door. She needed to escape for now, this was getting complicated and she was afraid of where it was leading.

As he closed the door behind her, Greg gave out a little groan and leaned against it for support. How on earth was he going to concentrate now?

"I think some food is in order," he mumbled to himself as he strode across the apartment to his kitchen. He hadn't eaten since breakfast and his stomach was unhappy with just coffee and the occasional bite out of an apple, he had had on the go all day.

As he flicked the kettle on, the silence was broken by the noises it made.

"Blasted noise," Greg said out loud. He had meant to buy a new one last time he went into town for supplies. Rummaging for a Post-it note, its bright luminescent pink sneaking out beneath the pile of papers he had on the side. Greg scribbled himself a note: "buy a kettle, razors and chocolate for cake." The hours had passed so quickly he had forgotten his line of thought, and his hunger was so apparent he could hear his tummy grumbling in anticipation. *Baked beans on toast it is then*, he thought to himself as he scanned the cupboards. Adding to his list, "buy more groceries before you starve."

Laughing to himself, he settled down at the table, pushing his computer to one side, his plate balancing on top of a steaming mug of coffee whilst his other hand dealt with the mess. The beautiful invitation Suzie had presented to him falling to the floor as he brushed aside the notebook that he had been frantically scribbling in, his thoughts for the next four chapters safely stowed away to be rekindled on the pages of his novel.

As he picked it up, he noticed the wording:

Crichton's Gala Dinner & Cocktail Party
Saturday 14th June 2014
The Great Room, Grosvenor House Hotel
Park Lane
18:30 champagne reception
19:30 dinner
Carriages at 01:30
R.S.V.P. Suzie Crichton (6562942)

Formal attire

Pure elegance, he thought to himself as he rested the card against his computer. Suzie's eye for detail was ever-present in the embossed card and scalloped edges. Its navy-blue wording standing out, proud to the touch.

He was imagining the splendour of it all. The Great Room he remembered from his last visit was exquisite and timeless. A far cry from his baked beans on toast. *It's time to brush off the old tux,* he thought to himself, *and have some fun*

Chapter 20

"Come on, darling!" he shouted down to Isabella, his eagerness for her to see their new home apparent by the huge smile on his face and his gesturing from the top floor window. Bobby had run up ahead to make sure everything was as it should be. The cleaners had promised him it would look spotless, and it did.

As the lift arrived inside the newly refurbished penthouse apartment, nestled on top of Telford Parade Mansions, Bobby couldn't help but smile at the sheer look of joy on his wife's face.

"Oh Robert, it's beautiful!" She beamed as he rushed forward to hug his beloved Isabella.

"It really is, isn't it?" He smiled back and took her hand for the grand tour.

All their beautiful furniture had been meticulously placed to show off its clean lines and homely features. Booby had taken charge when asked what was needed for the new apartment, choosing only the right combinations. The wrap-around leather sofa that swallowed you up in an instant. They loved to curl up on it and watch a movie on the giant sixty-inch TV. Many a time the kids would all be jammed on it too, for a family night of films and popcorn. The glass coffee table and side tables allowing as much light as possible to reflect around the room.

As Isabella walked from room to room, she slid her hand lovingly over the giant oak table that had been the centrepiece to many a dinner party and homework session alike. The tall dark brown leather chairs standing like soldiers around it, waiting for the next instalment.

Her much-loved dresser, yellow in colour with glass fronts, displaying in all its glory her 1930s Meakin. She had collected it her whole life, and it now had a home. She had bought the dresser at an old market in Suffolk and had lovingly restored it and painted it yellow. The wax overcoat just hinting at a shine. Now, it stood proudly in her new dining room for all to see.

Bobby held her hand so tightly it was as if he thought she would disappear if he let it go. He loved Isabella with all his heart, she knew that, didn't she? He knew he had not been completely faithful, but he always came home to her. That was his way of making it seem as though everything was just fine in their lives.

The bedroom, a vast sprawling suite really, looked like a hotel room. The silver and white flock on the walls as soft as a newly picked peach. The silk velvet drapes in the greyest steel, hanging effortlessly from the encased windows. A bed so large they could all fit in it; Isabella was sure that they would all be tucked up on a Sunday morning looking at the papers and their comics, chatting amongst themselves; the croissants and orange juice flowing and spilling with abandon. Her dressing room was large and filled with new closets and drawers all ready to be filled. And Isabella knew exactly where to go for some new lines. Hadn't Robert mentioned that Suzie Crichton lived in their building? She would make it her business to introduce herself, after all, Crichton's was one of her favourite labels, and weren't all the best dressed wearing it?

As Isabella gazed into the large mirror across from the bed, she could see her husband staring at her.

"Whatever is the matter?" she said as she crossed the room to take his hand again. "Come on, let's go and see the kitchen, and we can have a drink to celebrate before the children arrive with Winnie."

As Bobby took her hand, he wondered if life would ever be the same again. Would Isabella forgive this latest indiscretion, or was it all going to fall like a deck of cards thrown in the air?

"Robert, get the champagne glasses for me, and bring some for the children too. They will want a little glass of bubbles to cheers with us, I am sure." For now, Bobby had a reprieve; the magazine article wasn't due to be published for a few more days. *Who knows* he thought, *maybe they won't even go to print.*

Chapter 21

Winnie, their grandmother, never drank, but she allowed her "babies," as she called them, a little treat so long as they only had a little. After all, it was good for them; they needed to know that alcohol was a fact of life and handling it was a skill.

Her husband, Robert, had been a marvel. He couldn't drink that much as it made him sleepy, so Winnie was blessed with a man that always had an even temper and was so kind and generous to everyone. Bobby, on the other hand, had discovered drink at an early age and he loved nothing more than spending his wages on "beers for the boys," as he called it. How strange that he always seemed to have to buy his friends, unlike his father, whom people bent over backwards to be nearby. Their similarities ended with their looks.

As the lift rose through the majestic building like a phoenix out of the flames, the children could be heard chatting excitedly, eager to see their new home. Their rooms were already filled with their beloved books and toys, waiting for new memories to be made.

Winnie's eyes lit up as the concertina door was fully opened by her son, allowing her to take in the full expanse of the apartment. The children rushed out, and with glee, they ran to see their rooms. Isabella had commissioned name plaques to be installed on each door, making it easier for them to find their way.

Ava, Lilly and Harry, their coats already off and strewn across their bedroom floors, could be heard around the apartment.

"Oh, Mummy, I love my grown-up bedroom!" shouted Lilly. Having shared a room before with Amy, she was finally going to be able to spread out and have her own space. Their oldest daughter, Amy, was off at university and would surely love her room when she came home in the half term.

Lilly, thirteen years old and quite a girl, was never a sheep. With her very own style, Bobby chastised her for her sense of dress and individuality, but Isabella rejoiced in her refreshing outlook on life and how she wanted to live it. Her long brown hair tamed into so many different styles and always topped with a hat. Lilly was destined for great things in life and longed to be on the stage, just like her big sister.

As she walked around her room, feeling the beautiful fabrics on the bed and the soft furnishings, all vibrant colours and different textures, she imagined herself sprawled on the oversized bed, reading and drawing — her two favourite pastimes.

Harry, their only son, was more reserved. He didn't need to shout, as his father had chosen his fixtures and fittings, and he had all he needed. A sensible desk and swivel chair for his study. The tell-tale colours of blue and green that formed his walls and carpet were firm favourites, and everything was practical and tidy — much like Harry himself. He longed to go into the city when he was older and become a trader. He already had his life plan mapped out; Bobby and Isabella knew exactly where he was heading, and at sixteen, he was well on his way.

Ava was the baby of the family; she was a result of a very drunken night in the Bahamas seven years ago, an unexpected surprise and one that they had not bargained for. Her dark hair rolled in curls around her small chubby face as she ran from room to room too excited to stay put in her own.

"Daddy, I love it all. Thank you for my lovely room!" she bellowed as she literally ran straight into Winnie in the kitchen.

"Slow down, young lady," her grandmother chastised her darling granddaughter, smiling all the time as she could never be cross with her babies.

As the cork sprang from the bottle, the bubbles rushed out, all over Bobby's hand, splattering onto the beautiful Italian granite worktop and popping as they sprawled out across the impermeable surface. Bobby called all his children to him. The glasses charged, they all rose, and a big cheer rang out around the space,

"To our new family home!" said Bobby with a smile. As the bubbles jostled and danced about his nose, he took a large gulp and just for now relaxed into the beautiful surroundings. He had finally found his dream home.

Chapter 22

"Come on, darling, it's nearly five-thirty, and we have to be there by six at the latest," Suzie shouted across the hallway to Max, who was procrastinating over which shoes to wear with his tuxedo. There really wasn't any choice; he had bought a lovely pair of Jeffery West shoes that epitomised pure elegance. As he slipped them onto his feet, he could smell the smooth dark leather, its lustre shining up at him.

"All set," he called back, giving himself a final check in the long mirror inside his dressing room.

The Great Room held many gala dinners, but this was the party of the year. The who's who in the fashion and modelling world had RSVP'd and Suzie would be centre stage for all to see. The opulence of the five-star setting, drenched in history and being located on Park Lane in London, was going to be the talk of the town; every newspaper editor was pen poised to hit the headlines first.

A beautiful red carpet stretched out onto the pavement, adorned with strung lights and rope barriers to keep the photographers and tourists back, allowing the grand entrance to be the focal point for all to see.

What a sight they were going to make. Suzie and Max were first to arrive, the hosts of the evening, and in Suzie's case, the star of the show. Her collaboration with the Jordan & Cleeve brand had been hushed to a whisper until the right time to announce it in the press had arrived, causing a wave of excitement across the industry and a chain reaction of events that led to this very night.

Her gown, the colour of cornflowers, fitted where it touched and hugged her small frame as if it were moulded to her body. *Thank God I haven't eaten anything more than salad for the last few weeks*, she thought to herself, as she remembered the glorious sensations that Greg's cakes had delivered to her senses. The pewter shoes she had picked up as a bargain buy from a little boutique just up the road from her studio matched impeccably with the bag that her good friend Kelly Gale had given her. She had received it as a freebie from the Victoria's Secret fashion show in December, and they went hand in glove together. With nothing more than her diamond stud earrings, the bodice of the dress was encrusted with bugle beads that shone like shards of ice against the lights, and as she always said, "less is more!"

Their entrance was grand as they stepped from the sleek black limousine that Mary Cleeve had insisted on ordering. The bulbs around them flashed and danced, with each photographer wanting to capture every angle of the gown as Suzie and Max walked the red carpet towards the biggest night of both of their lives, in more ways than one.

Chapter 23

As the guests arrived, the reception hall soon began to fill, and Suzie lost sight of Max. Where on earth, did he keep disappearing to? Little did she know that the appearance of his assistant had set him into a tailspin, as he had no idea that Holly was invited, let alone had accepted. In her ice-blue gown, which matched her eyes, she looked the part of a model from head to foot. How was he going to concentrate on his wife with his mistress in attendance?

The champagne was flowing faster than the waiters could keep up! Who knew that the fashion world could drink more than their body weights in alcohol?

Mary Cleeve arrived with a rush of excitement and noise, the photographers jumping the ropes to get as close as they could. Dressed elegantly in one of her own creations, a black taffeta A-line that accentuated her slender body and complimented her husband Jordan's tuxedo. His bow tie, not black but a pale shade of green, brought out the flecks of green in his eyes. Walking hand in hand across the red carpet, they looked every inch the celebrity couple. Jordan cheekily pulled up his right trouser leg to show off his pale green socks with a wink, making Mary laugh as they walked.

As the doors opened, The Great Room came into view, the Master of Ceremonies hailing the guests to their seats. The linens in sky-blue, accented by turquoise, were folded and swirled into glasses. The crystal shone. and the chandeliers sparkled in the glory of it all. Suzie gasped inwardly as her vision came to life in front of her.

Seated at the same table as Mary and Jordan, her eyes searched the room for Greg. Was he here? Had he taken up the invitation? Did he come alone? So many questions were running through her head, and still no sightings of Max.

He was chasing after Holly, but she was far too busy. Her attentions were firmly set on David Summers and his companions; his eyes drinking in her beauty, the ice in her eyes catching every light that was above her. The group of people he was with were familiar. Max recognised Laura Nelson; he remembered she used to be with Steven from apartment number three. Who was that she was with? Tall, mousey brown hair, and a washboard stomach apparent through his slim-fit shirt. He had seen him on a morning TV show, he seemed to remember. And was that Bobby Collier from the top floor? Wow, his wife was stunning. He recognised her from the news; she was a big-shot divorce lawyer who took people to the cleaners.

As the final call came up to be seated, Max turned on his heels and strode across the dance floor towards the top table. Suzie, her mousey blonde hair framing her face, eyes so dark blue they were like pools you could swim in, and her elegance paramount, as everyone's glances were of appreciation and envy. Seeing him heading her way, her smile widened and her arms opened in wait of his embrace. His rejection was apparent for all to see. As Suzie lowered her arms, she spun around and started to chat to Jordan, his knowing eyes showing her he would be there for her. She would deal with Max tomorrow; her night wasn't going to be spoiled by him. Not ever.

The first course was divine: a delicate plate of smoked salmon rolled into roses on a bed of fresh crisp greens. The vibrant spattering of baby plum tomatoes adding a flavour like no other, complemented by a sharp, creamy lemon dressing. It looked so good it was a shame to eat it, but eat it she did. Suzie had forgotten lunch and was feeling rather faint after the two glasses of champagne on a literally empty stomach. Her conversations across the table were light and easy, and she soon settled into having a good time with the people in her life that really mattered.

Mary Cleeve stood as the first course was cleared, and with a silver knife, its mother of pearl handle glittering in her hand, tapped gently but with vigour the side of her cut crystal champagne glass. The room came to a gentle hush and all eyes were on her. As she talked, she thanked her husband and her close colleagues for their support across the years, taking nothing away from him and his part in her growing success. The stories she portrayed of an industry filled with beautiful clothes, people and places had the whole attention of the venue; even the waiters stood and listened to her softly spoken words.

She introduced Suzie to speak, and the room burst into applause and cheers for the lady behind Crichton's, the name on everyone's lips tonight. As Suzie rose to her feet, she caught sight of Greg, his hazel eyes fixed firmly on her; the smile on his face showing her how happy he was for her. As he brushed aside an ebony curl that had escaped and was trying its hardest to obscure his vision, he gave her a tiny little wave. Nobody else noticed, but Suzie saw, and this one little gesture spurred her on, and she began to speak.

The next five minutes were a whirl of thanks and gratitude to all who were involved in Crichton's. Jordan and Mary were ever present in her musings, and she was soon sitting back down as the Master of Ceremonies announced there would be a musical interlude before the main course was served. Rising to her feet, Suzie needed to stretch her legs, and there was nowhere else that she wanted to be than at Greg's table.

Seeing her walk away, Max headed towards Holly's table. His stride was urgent, and as he took off his jacket, his lean body was visible through the sheer, crisp white fabric. Throwing it over his shoulder, he brought attention to himself, and all eyes were on him. As Holly spotted him coming, she laid a hand on David's arm and moved in a little closer. Her intention was to make Max jealous, and from the look on his face, it was working. As he neared the table, his temper was piqued, and he was oblivious to what was unfolding around him. He grabbed her hand, and snatched her up from the table, pulling her into him, and kissing her hard.

"Keep your hands off my girl," he said to David.

"Pay attention to your own date!" he shouted as he tried to pull Holly away from the table. All the while, Suzie's eyes were ever present on the scene. She had her doubts about Max for a while, and this was the final nail in the coffin for them

Holly pulled away and glanced about her.

"Max, remember where you are." His attention firmly on Holly, he didn't take any notice.

"You are mine, and mine alone!" he was shouting now.

"Music, please," the Master of Ceremonies was calling for more music. "Please dance everyone, while we wait for the next course." As people were ushered to the dance floor, Max and Holly headed for the stairs, sweeping up onto the main concourse above The Great Room. As the party carried on without them, the gentle chatter sweeping around the room, Suzie brushed down her dress, and without a moment's hesitation, she asked Greg to dance.

Chapter 24

Number two was a hive of activity as they were getting ready to welcome the new additions. Anna had been right; Lizzie was having a baby, and Isaac couldn't believe it when she finally did the test. With all the sickness and nausea, she eventually went to the doctors and he confirmed that no, she wasn't poorly, she was in fact pregnant.

The twelve-week scan had been a revelation as they all huddled around the monitor Isaac, Anna and Joseph all there for moral support, the radiographer turned with a huge smile on his face and said without hesitation, "Its twins! Wow, there are two in there, and all this time you thought you were expecting one."

Isaac nearly fainted with the shock and Lizzie began to cry. *How are they going to cope?* she thought to herself.

Her mother-in-law, suspecting the fear, laid her hand over Lizzie's and said, "Don't worry, darling, Joseph and I will help." It was time to let the boys know that they were no longer going to be active parts of the business. They had a new job as grandparents.

As the room was cleared, ready for the two cots and baby monitor that Anna had purchased especially for the new babies, it was time to install all the beautiful soft furnishings and furniture that Suzie had helped Anna pick out on their last visit into town. The new nursery in the Rosenberg's apartment was a welcome addition; it meant that Isaac could concentrate on the business and Lizzie would have all the help she needed with the twins. They, of course, had their own room at home, but this was to help out, to be part of the family and be the grandparents they needed to be. They hadn't been able to help Luther and Ada when they started their family; the business was too consuming. But they had all talked and agreed that Lizzie needed the help, and Isaac and Luther could then tend to the business. Rosenberg's was being handed over to the next generation, and things were going to have to change.

Chapter 25

The party was in full swing, and Suzie was busily chatting to her guests. The excitement from before soon forgotten with the meal being served and the music starting. Greg had told her how beautiful she looked, and she had danced the night away, loving the attention and the ease being with him brought.

Having talked to almost everyone in the room, she was physically and mentally exhausted. The need to just relax and be free of the pressures put upon her was overwhelming, and Suzie just wanted to go home. Isabella Collier caught her eye as she was heading for the stairs.

"Hello Suzie. I have wanted to chat to you all night." Suzie stopped in her tracks and graciously held out her hand. "I just moved into the penthouse apartment at the Mansion."

"Oh, hello," Suzie said, "I was wondering if it was you. Isabella Collier, divorce lawyer to the stars!" Suzie beamed.

Isabella flung her head back in laughter and smiled the loveliest smile, "Yes, that's me, if only I could take my own advice."

Suzie started up the stairs and promised Isabella a proper chat over a glass of bubbles very soon. Greg was waiting for her in the foyer, her coat in hand.

"Come on, lovely lady," he said, "let's get you home and tucked up in bed." Suzie squeezed his hand and allowed him to lead her out the front of the hotel and into a waiting taxi.

As they sped through the streets of London, they sat in silence, the gentle hum of the engine the only noise between them. Greg could feel the tension in the car but said nothing. The journey wasn't long, and they would soon be home.

The lights were all off in the Mansion House as they approached. Their beloved building looked so regal amongst its surroundings. Suzie had no idea if Max had gone home; she assumed he hadn't. The lobby was a welcome sight, and as Greg led her towards number one, she allowed his arm to circle her waist. As they strode in time, there was nowhere else she would rather be.

How many times had she been in his apartment, and it was only now that she could take in the furniture he possessed and his taste in accessories? The library table with its red leather top, a sideboard adorned with the prettiest crystal decanters, and was that a gramophone in the corner? This man had great taste, and it suited him. His apartment suited him.

As she walked around his sitting room, her fingers brushed across the surfaces, picking up photographs of family members, she assumed. She could feel the stresses of the day falling away. As she turned to talk to Greg, he was already upon her, two brandy glasses in hand, the golden liquid slipping up the sides of the glass as he swirled them in his hands. Passing one to Suzie, he raised his glass to hers, and as their glasses chinked, he took her hand and led her to the sumptuous burgundy Chesterfield sofa, its buttons pulling every inch of it as tight as a drum. As they sat, Suzie sipped her drink and took in the deep hazel eyes that were searching her face for a sign, any sign that this was where she wanted to be. She laid her glass on the mahogany coffee table, and without saying a word, she leaned in and kissed Greg, softly at first, then with an urgency that they both felt come alive between them.

Suzie stopped and said, "Are you sure you want to do this?" And with a sweep of his arm, he pulled her to him, ever gentle and so sensual she felt as if she would burst. *This is going to be a long night*, she thought to herself as she closed her eyes and allowed him to take her to places she had never been before.

Chapter 26

Waterloo Station, under the clock at eleven a.m. Easy, she could do that. Wearing her black jeans, a crisp white t-shirt, and her beloved Barbour jacket with the Liberty print running through the inside, Isabella pulled on her new purple Vans, checked herself for one last time in the hall mirror, and headed out into the sunshine. Comfortable shoes, that's what she needed for the endless walking up and down Oxford Street, looking for that perfect bargain. Amy, her daughter, loved to shop. Isabella always said that was the gene she never got, which brought about much laughter. But it was true, shopping was a chore for her, not a pleasure.

What a fantastic day. The leaves on the trees were just turning from their dark green to the burnt amber and brown hues that made her realise how soon winter would be here and her fifty-first birthday.

The tube journey passed without much drama. A small boy sang the alphabet song and played I Spy as the train trundled through the many stations, their brightly coloured posters flashing by, unseen and failing to impress.

The escalator down to the main concourse was packed, and the station seemed to be overflowing with jostling people, too busy in their own journeys to notice a casually dressed lady with nothing better to do than meet for lunch and shop. Well, that was the impression she wanted to give off today.

The large clock floated like a majestic eagle in the air, looking down on all the passers-by. Ten thirty and too early just to stand, so she found herself browsing the greetings card stand inside the newsagents, not looking for anything in particular to buy, just enjoying being able to forget what was going on at home and immerse herself into the hustle and bustle of the journey.

Isabella and Amy had joked about wearing a carnation so they could recognise each other, like a scene from an old Spencer Tracy movie. That had made them laugh so hard, Isabella really missed the laughter and joy that her older daughter brought to her life.

Amy had left home to forge her own life at university, studying performing arts and loving every minute of the social and performing side of it all. She worked for hours on lavish costumes and splendid props as a way of making her own way. She didn't want to just rely on her parents for everything.

Isabella found herself wondering where all the different people were going. There was the lady with the veil on and her happy entourage — a hen do! That would be messy later, she smiled to herself. A young boy tugging at his mother's sleeve, vying for her attention. Her phone gripped so tightly in her hand, she was completely oblivious to her child's needs and carried on texting and laughing as if he didn't exist.

Out of the corner of her eye she could see a man wondering towards her, a book in his hand. *Oh no, not a Jehovah's Witness*, she thought, *that's all I need.* As he drew closer, Isabella saw that he was smiling and he held a novel in his hands.

"You're not carrying a book," he said.

"No," she said, feeling a little puzzled. "Should I be?"

"You're not the one I am waiting for, are you?" he said, looking so forlorn you would think that he had just been given some very sad news.

"No, I don't think so," she said with the smile that always came from her heart. With that, the silver-haired stranger sighed, dropped his eyes and turned to leave, saying what a shame that was. She could see him shaking his head from side to side as he stretched ahead to watch from his vantage point.

Isabella felt as if her heart would break. Who was this man, and why did he choose her to share a smile with that day? As a fifty-year-old woman, she had no assumptions about her looks, her weight, or how other people saw her. Always confident and capable, she didn't need that constant reassurance.

As she saw her daughter approaching, her beautiful dress flowing and the classic Dr Martens she so loved to wear bounding towards her, all thoughts of the stranger were gone for now. Amy stretched out her arms and embraced her Mum, drinking in the scent of the Chanel No 5 she so loved to wear. That was the smell that made Amy know she was safe. She remembered her mother scooping her up as a child to blow raspberries on her tummy, the smell ever present and welcoming. As they parted and linked arms, both smiling from ear to ear, they headed off to the tube in search of the best bargains in town.

The sun was shining brightly as they emerged up the steps and out into the bustle of Oxford Circus. Both squinting as they brushed past shoppers jostling both up and down the steps.

Isabella, her eyes always darting, making sure that she didn't bump into anyone, caught sight of a news stand on the other side of the pavement. Her mouth wide open, she tried to steer Amy away from the sight before her. Surely not, he hadn't, not again!

Amy saw her mother's expression and as her eyes scanned the scene before them, she couldn't quite believe what she was seeing. There, on the front of a glossy magazine, was her father. He was kissing a very beautiful blonde, half his age, with big ice-blue eyes and a sky-blue dress on. *What the hell? she was as young as Amy!*

"Oh my god, Mum," Amy shrieked as her mother took her hand and led her across the busy road and into a café that was so full of noise and distractions that neither of them could speak.

Chapter 27

Isaac and Luther settled into running their parents' business with ease. Side by side, they stepped up and into their respective roles. Luther, being the eldest and more adapted to family life, took the reins as the head of the company, with Isaac as his very close second. With Lizzie and the twins on his mind, Luther needed to be in control to carry the business forward.

He had been planning a collaboration with a new designer for a while, and on meeting Suzie Crichton at a corporate party, he had been so impressed by her and the ability she had to turn heads in a room full of women. Now he was on his way to her studio in Covent Garden, feeling both excited and nervous to be taking such a large step for Rosenberg's. Luther knew that this would change the face of his parents' company, hopefully for the best.

"Luther, come on in," Suzie greeted him with her usual smile and a firm handshake. She had always been taught to shake a hand, showing the recipient that you meant business. N*othing worse than limp wrists and sweaty palms* her mother had always said. "Can I get you anything, tea or coffee"? Luther smiled and said he was fine, and they settled down opposite each other in her little office. She had never felt the need for a grand space; she felt at home in there with her samples of fabric scattered here and there, scribblings and ideas on anything she could find at the time, and its beautiful saffron walls that made feel warm and cosy on even the chilliest of days. This was where she did all her thinking, not only about her own business and how she could improve it, but many an hour was whiled away thinking about Max and what on earth she was going to do about the handsome Greg.

Bringing herself back to Luther, Suzie was intrigued about his visit. He had said that he wanted to talk to her about taking Rosenberg's in a different direction style wise, and he would love her input. Little did she realise that it was more than her input he needed, he was asking her to design a whole new line for them and he wanted the three companies to unite in the venture; Jordan & Cleeve, Rosenberg's and Crichton's all working together to create something magical. Suzie's designs, his cutters and finishers and Jordan & Cleeve handling the worldwide distribution. It could work for all of them if they put their heads together and made the right plans.

Rosenberg's usual bespoke business needed a shake up and bringing into the current century. Less and less people were having suits made, and off the peg although already being established within Rosenberg's it needed to be heading in a more up market direction.

But not any old clothes they had to scream style and if they were to have the Rosenberg's seal of approval would have to have the wow factor.

Luther jumped straight on in, no need to skirt around the issue and his ideas for this collaboration. She was a tour de force and he knew without a shadow of a doubt that this was going to be the best opportunity to send Rosenberg's into the heart and minds of the fashion world. As a planner and a list maker, he unfolded his ideas and scribbled wildly as they came to him, in his big blue book, he could see the look of excitement on Suzie's face.

"So, let me get this straight, you want me to design a line for you"? As Luther nodded, he couldn't help but smile. "Then we use your pattern makers, cutters and finishers, and then who distributes?" In Luther's mind this was where Jordan & Cleeve came in. They had the contacts and the systems in place for mass distribution, surely, they would jump at the chance of adding to their already lucrative lines. As he explained his thoughts to Suzie, it all made absolute sense.

"Fabulous idea Luther," Suzie said as she got up to walk around the room. She thought more clearly when she could walk and talk. It's a win-win situation for all involved, and I am sure Mary Cleeve will be delighted when she sees all your plans and ideas.

Luther, getting to his feet, felt elated as he crossed the room. He caught sight of himself in the full-length mirror; he looked sharp in his Rosenberg's original and felt confident that his own sense of style would pay dividends going forward. If he and Suzie were going to forge a long-standing business arrangement, they both had to be on the same page for the designs and final finishes of the new Rosenberg's products.

Chapter 28

As they stood outside the hotel, waiting for Laura's car to arrive, Nick tried his hardest to look like he wanted to be there. He had escorted her to the event because she had asked him, unbeknown to her, he had his own agenda.

Climbing into the limousine, Laura stretched out her long legs and slipped off her Giuseppe Zanotti Peony sandals. Their black satin ankle strap falling away to reveal her beautifully pedicured toes.

"Come on, darling, get in and rub my feet for me." As obedient as ever Nick climbed in and did as he was told. After all, how was he going to get what he needed without a little bit of discomfort?

Living in a small block of flats not too far from Park Lane, she was earning a six-figure salary, so had treated herself to exactly what she wanted. On the second floor of a beautiful old Victorian block, there were two bedrooms and the biggest dressing room she had ever seen. As they pulled up, she told her driver not to wait and ushered Nick out of the car and into her flat.

Nick had to work fast, he needed to set up his camera before Laura realised what he was doing. As she went through her usual routine of taking off her make-up and brushing out her hair, he got to work. She needed a shower, and Nick knew exactly what to do. He worked speedily, and as he pushed the record button, he knew that this was the final take on this kiss and tell. Laura Nelson was never going to know what hit her, well not tonight anyway.

"So, my love, what is it that you need from me?" Nick, ever thoughtful, pulled Laura into his arms and planted a smattering of kisses across her nose, making her shudder a little in surprise. What were these feelings? This was Nick; she didn't want Nick, did she? As she brought her thoughts back to the job at hand, she needed to brush all thoughts of her feelings aside. She needed a trainer and Nick was going to do it. She had always managed to manipulate him; whatever she wanted, he gave her.

"Darling," she drawled as she released herself from Nick's warm and inviting arms. "Sit and talk a littl.e I want to know everything that has been going on with you," she said as she patted the sofa beside where she had perched herself, allowing Nick to see her long legs, just enough of her thigh showing to catch his attention.

As they chatted, it was like the old days when they were young and carefree. They slipped back into their old ways and Laura found herself yielding to him. Nick was handsome; he had grown into himself, and his physique was all that and more. His Armani t-shirt hugged every contour of his upper body and his Levi jeans showed off his muscular legs, groaning under the pressure of the taught thigh muscles encased in them. His shoes kicked off at the door gave way to bare feet, beautifully tanned and manicured toes. *He really looks after himself,* she thought, all the while raising her eyes back to his, to let him know she was hanging on his every word.

She had missed this; she had missed him. The feeling of loss and longing hit her like a sledgehammer. He had been there all along, her whole life, and she had treated him so badly. Now, on the verge of using him again, she found herself backtracking to find the right words to express herself.

All the while, the video was recording and seeing them both, like a voyeur watching in, waiting for the pain and suffering to begin. Instead, being treated to the most electrifying expression of love and lust between two people that could ever be seen. What was going on? Nick's plan of a kiss and tell was not going according to plan. Did this woman actually like him? Was she truly feeling what he thought she was?

Floating as if she were on cloud nine, Laura headed for her perfect little kitchen in the flat. It was pristine; she never cooked a thing, and her refrigerator was filled with champagne and not much else. As she reached in to grasp a bottle, she felt him behind her. The phone was switched off as he passed it, and all thoughts of his deception were long gone. His arm circled her waist and spun her around to face him. His eyes searching hers for a response that she was feeling the same. As Laura placed the bottle on the oak worktop, she felt him lift her into his arms, and the kiss was exquisite. It was not the fumbling of youth that she remembered, but the tender, soft, sensual kiss of a well-practiced lover. After all, Nick wasn't a boy any longer. He tasted of spearmint and smelt of Aramis, so damn sexy she literally didn't know what hit her.

He strode with ease across the flat, and taking her direction, headed for the bedroom. It was a beautiful room, its crimson walls inviting them in as he gently laid her on the over-sized bed. Its six hundred thread count cotton sheets feeling like silk beneath her. As he bent down ever so teasingly to open her nightgown, the tie belt lightly knotted so it fell away easily. His gaze was forever on her face, wanting to see her every expression. As he allowed his eyes to roam, he took in a breath. He had dreamed of this for years and his growing desire was ever apparent.

Their lovemaking was sensual, not rushed. He took his time, always asking what she wanted, if it was good for her, ever thoughtful of what she wanted. Her responses to him were welcomed with a heightened pleasure that he had never felt before. As they lay there, their bodies entwined, Laura thought about how amazing he was, and she never wanted that feeling to end.

Gently, Nick eased himself away from her and knew without a shadow of a doubt he could never hurt her, not ever. Leaning up on one elbow, he couldn't take his eyes off her. Her smile was captivating and he all but drowned in the green of her eyes. He had never seen such a colour before, contrasting the auburn of her hair; she was perfect.

"Can I jump in your shower?" he smiled wickedly, as he got off the bed and strode away, not waiting for the reply. Laura Nelson, the tears prickling her eyes, couldn't help but smile and thought to herself about all the wasted years and how horrid she had been to her best friend Nick.

Scooting out of bed, she rushed after him, her naked body glistening from their lovemaking.

"Is there room in there for two?" she chuckled and without hesitation stepped in and closed the door behind her. As she kissed him, she couldn't help but think about all the feelings that she had never had before, never felt before, not with Steven or anyone. Was she in love with Nick? He already knew that he loved her with all his heart, no matter what their history; Nick loved Laura!

Chapter 29

Amy, taking her mother's hand, said with a whisper, "Mum, what the hell was that?" As they retrieved their skinny lattes from the counter, they headed towards an empty table as far away from the entrance as Isabella could find. Her thoughts were reeling at what they had just witnessed. Thinking that everyone was looking at her, she felt as if she wanted the floor to open up and swallow her.

"Let me gather my thoughts, my dear girl. I hoped you and all our children would be spared his infidelities." Amy looked on in wonder. Had her dad her beloved dad done this before? Was this not news to her Mum?

"Who is she Mum?" Amy found herself saying with a little too much panic in her voice.

Her mum's soothing voice came back as a whisper. "I don't know, my darling, but this is the final straw He has gone too far this time."

They sat for what seemed like an age, sipping their drinks and just letting it all sink in. Isabella had let things slip, had let him have his fun, and this is how he repays her. Stay together for the children, isn't that what people do? Well, her children were the most precious thing in her life, and she would not stand by and let Robert Collier destroy their lives.

"What are we going to do Mum?" Amy said, close to tears as the prospect hit her so hard it took her breath away. "Are you and Dad going to get a divorce?" The word caught in her throat as the tears came, and Isabella, being ever the mum, put her own feelings aside to soothe and ease the pain that her eldest daughter was feeling.

"It will all be okay, you know. We will work this out and make it as painless as possible for you all." As Isabella said the words, she knew without a shadow of a doubt that her marriage was over, and she knew how to get exactly what her and her children deserved. Her mind processed all his mistakes, as he called them, over the years. Did he really think that it would never come to an end? Isabella had to get on this as soon as possible. She could see the headlines now: "Top Divorce Lawyer to the Stars: Is it all over for Isabella and Robert Collier?"

Chapter 30

The twins arrived on a cold November morning, just as Isaac was setting off for a meeting with a supplier. Lizzie had been looking anxious all morning. As he stepped out the door, he saw the look of sheer terror on her face.

"What's the matter, my beautiful one?" he was always so thoughtful with how he addressed his wife; after all, he was a very lucky man.

"I feel a little strange," Lizzie said as she steadied herself in the doorway.

Isaac, seeing his wife was in distress, turned on his heels, made a quick call to the supplier, and headed back into their little home.

"Come on, sit down and I will call the midwife." As Isaac picked up the phone, he was worried. There were four weeks to go, and this was too early, surely.

As the midwife was literally just around the corner, she was there in no time.

"Now Isaac, make yourself useful and put the kettle on," she winked at Lizzie as her husband went off to do as he was told. "Now let's take a look at you Lizzie," she said with a smile that made her relax just a little.

"Well, I think it's time," she said as she removed the gloves from her hands, making sure to dispose of them into a sealed bag.

"Let me," Isaac said as he took the rubbish from her hands and made his exit into the kitchen. He needed to steady himself. After all, it wasn't every day that you became a father. As he busied himself collecting the suitcase that had been sitting by the bedroom door for the last four weeks, he remembered his brother. He was a mess with his first child.

The trip to the hospital was swift and steady, the cold wind outside an unwelcome visitor in the car, but Lizzie needed the air. She was feeling very frightened and excited all at once. Two babies were going to be a hard task. *We can do it though, can't we?* She thought to herself.

Isaac had called Luther and his parents; they said they would be there when they could and wished him and Lizzie good luck. Ada had sent a text message saying she would meet them there. She and Lizzie were very close, like sisters really, and she wanted to be there, even if it was just outside the room. On arrival, Lizzie was assessed, and they confirmed that she was already four centimetres dilated, and they were going to break her waters. *Surely that should happen first?* Lizzie thought to herself, but she was in their hands, and after all, babies are born every minute of every day.

Monitors were set up, birth plan in place, and as the contractions got closer together, Isaac could see that it was getting closer to the point of labour. They had practiced this in every class they went to, and he was trying very hard to be there and do what Lizzie asked of him. The ice chips to cool her down and keep her hydrated were a huge welcome, and Lizzie used the gas and air with ease.

"This is great stuff," she said to Isaac as another contraction gripped her.

The midwife, ever present, was readying herself for the imminent labour and advising Lizzie on what was going to happen and that it was going to be hard work. Isaac was in awe of this amazing creature as she pushed their babies out into the world. As the first baby crowned, the midwife asked Lizzie to stop.

"One last push," she said. And as she did Isaac could see the first sight of their newly born son. He looked perfect, and as he cut the cord, they whisked him away to weigh and check he was doing okay.

Lizzie was resting, and as the midwife said, "Here we go again," Lizzie looked exhausted but got the energy from somewhere to push the second baby out. He came out like Superman, his hand raised by his face as he almost flew into the world. Lizzie was overwhelmed as she allowed the tears to flow.

"We did it," she said to Isaac.

"No, darling, you did it. They both look perfect." Both babies wrapped in blue blankets and handed to their mother and father. This was a moment that they would never forget, and life would certainly never be the same again.

As the last stages of labour were carried out, Isaac went out into the corridor where Ada was waiting, an anxious look on her face.

"Two beautiful boys, they are perfect; ten fingers and ten toes each and the blackest hair," he said as Ada looked on, the biggest smile on her face. She pulled Isaac to her, and she felt him yield to her, the hug a much-needed release of tension.

Luther and his parents arrived as they were allowed back into Lizzie's room. The chatter and excitement causing the nurses to look up from their station.

"Well now isn't this a large group?" said the head nurse. "Please be mindful of Mum and what she has just done." As they took turns visiting the new babies and new parents, the world was a happier place, and the prospects for the future were ever rosier for them all.

Anna looked down at her two new grandsons with pride.

"Any names yet?" she said to nobody in particular.

"Joseph and Joshua, after their two grandfathers," Lizzie spoke with certainty as Isaac just looked on and nodded in agreement. The next generation of Rosenberg boys had fitting names and were surrounded with love.

Chapter 31

Suzie raced down the steps two at a time, her need to see him apparent on her face for all to see. Anna was perched on her chair outside number two; a book laid gently in her lap, her eyes closed just for a moment, her mind drifting to far-gone places and times. Joseph was there in her dreams as the young, handsome man she had fallen in love with. The book she was reading had taken her back to memories of her own past, and she smiled inwardly as she remembered the joy she had felt when her lovely, shy, adoring Joseph had proposed.

She opened her eyes as she heard Suzie coming.

"Sorry, Anna," Suzie said with the broadest smile on her face. Anna just nodded and looked towards Suzie's destination. The smile crept across her face as she noticed the door was open, and what was that amazing aroma? *Cinnamon and freshly baked bread,* she thought to herself. Suzie ran over to Anna, bent down as if talking to a small child, and took one of her delicate hands in hers. The skin felt like thin tissue paper, her age clearly visible from her hands alone. *No amount of cream could take away the years of toil from these hands,* she thought to herself.

"Thank you, Anna, for always being here, for taking care of us all, and for, well, just being you." As she stood up, she could see Joseph coming down the hallway of their resplendent apartment, and as she raised her hand to say hello, she turned her attention to her next stop: Number one, her final destination for the day, she hoped.

She could smell the baking from upstairs, and it was just one of the things she loved about Greg. After the other night, she knew that their friendship was more than that, and she wanted to see where this journey was going to take her. Max had made himself ever so clear the night of the party, and her lawyer was dealing with him now; she never wanted to see him again as long as she lived.

The door, already open, had a little note pinned to it. "Help yourself to a cinnamon swirl, I am in the shower. See you in a minute, Greg."

Suzie unpinned the note and shut the door behind her. The smell coming from his kitchen was unbelievable. A wire rack sat on the kitchen table, set neatly in rows like little soldiers were the smallest cinnamon swirls Suzie had ever seen. Literally two bites big, and they were still warm. As Suzie took the first bite, her senses went into overdrive. This wasn't just a bun; it was an adventure. The sensual aroma mixed with the exquisite flavours and danced inside her mouth like a slow-burning Rumba being stepped out on her tongue. The drizzle of icing so delicate you could hardly see it, oh, but it was there in the background with just a hint of sweetness to bring the delectable adventure to an end. Scanning the room, she noticed that the table was laid: two cups and saucers, two side plates, and the most delicate napkins she had ever seen. The sugar bowl and milk jug sat splendidly to one side, the stars of the show. Their art deco shape reminding her of bygone years as she mused at the thoughts of who had used them in the past and the stories they could tell. If only they could come to life just for a day!

The smell of after shave and soap made Suzie turn around with a start. She hadn't heard Greg pad from the bathroom to the kitchen, his bare feet making his arrival a silent one. His towel in his hand, rubbing at his ebony curls, water dripping onto his face, and his hazel eyes shining like pebbles in a pool, she rose to her feet, eager to touch this beautiful man. Wearing nothing but his signature grey bottoms, he looked divine. His wet skin catching the light from overhead, showing off every contour of his upper body. Suzie felt her skin tingle as they got closer, and she closed her eyes as he lowered his head to kiss her expertly on her lips. The gentlest kiss she had ever felt, making her whole body shudder in delight.

"You helped yourself, I see," Greg said as he brushed a small crumb of cinnamon-infused swirl from the corner of her mouth.

"I couldn't help myself," she said with the sweetest smile she could muster. "After all, you said I could in your note," she said as she lifted the note and waved it in front of him. Both of them stopping to laugh and enjoy the easiness between them.

"You having writers block again?" she said without thinking.

"No, actually, I was experimenting for Jessica, Steven's fiancée. She is gluten-free, so I said I would try and make her a treat."

"You are so kind and thoughtful, Greg Samuels," she almost sang out the words.

Ever the gentleman, he just raised his eyebrow and said, "That's me, what you see is what you get."

Was this man too good to be true? *Who knows,* Suzie thought to herself and she lowered herself into the balloon-backed dining chair and started to pour the tea for them both. The pretty 1930s china he had inherited from his grandmother took pride — of place between them. It was like being transported back to another era. This man enchanted her, and he had no problem at all sharing his treasures with her.

"After all," he said, "What is the point of having all these beautiful things, if you never use them?"

Recipe Three — Gluten free Cinnamon Swirls (Rebel Baker)

Dough mixture:
240 mL Almond milk
75 g White sugar

9–10 g dry yeast
460 g gluten free flour (Bobs Red Mill)
¼ teaspoon of salt
75 g coconut cream

For the filling:
40 g coconut cream
125 g castor sugar
1-2 teaspoons cinnamon

For the topping:
110 g coconut cream
40 g icing sugar

Method:

Mix warm milk, sugar, yeast & 2 spoons of flour, whisking lightly to relieve the lumps. Leave to stand for 5 minutes.

Add the flour, yeast & salt to the mixing bowl, and with the kneading hook, start kneading. When nearly mixed, add the coconut cream. Leave to stand for 15 minutes. The mixture should be slightly sticky. Transfer the dough to prove/rise in lightly floured bowl and cover with cling film. Leave for 1 hour or until it is doubled in size.

Prepare and butter an 11-inch baking dish.

Once the dough is doubled in size, transfer it onto a floured work surface and roll the dough to an 18 x 9-inch rectangle. Spread 2 – 3 spoons of coconut cream across the dough and sprinkle generously the cinnamon sugar mixture over the top. Gently rub the sugar into the cream; this will prevent spillages as it is rolled. Roll the dough tightly, lengthwise, and seal the bottom edge. Cut into 1.5-inch slices. Place in the buttered pan and cover with cling film. Leave for 45 – 60 minutes to rise.

Bake for 25 – 30 minutes until golden brown.

For the topping, mix the coconut cream and the icing sugar and drizzle over the still warm buns

Chapter 32

"Isabella, stop!" Bobby shouted as he tried to grab her by the hand.

"Not now; I am not ready to talk to you, Robert". She always called him Robert, to her, it was a grown-up name, and she couldn't take him seriously when their friends called him Bobby. "I would say talk to my lawyer, but I am my lawyer, so go away, Rober.t Get out of this apartment and away from me and the children." He didn't deserve to be listened to again, his endless lies and betrayal to both her and the children had come to an end. Robert Collier was going to rue the day he first ever cheated on them.

As she heard the lift door close behind him, the concertina gate making a welcoming sound of his departure, she headed for her closet. Filled with beautiful designs from the Crichton's range, which one to choose today? After all, Isabella had an important meeting to attend today. Suzie had hired her to finalise her divorce from Max. She had forged a friendship with Suzie that she knew would never be broken. Remembering the pain in Suzie's eyes on the night of the party, Isabella vowed then that she just had to help this incredible woman. She didn't deserve what Max had put her through! If only Isabella could take her own advice, she would have been free of Robert years ago.

It is so right what they say, *you can't help who you fall in love with*. With those words ringing in her ears, she headed for the lift; its elegant structure the focal point of her apartment. *How many people had travelled in that lift,* she thought to herself as she pulled across the bronzed clanking gate and encapsulated herself in the amazing 1930's splendour? The trip to the lobby was a mere minute or two, but she felt as if she were being whisked into another world. From her vantage point, she could see the doorways to the other apartments. *What were Steven and Jessica up to today,* she mused, with the idea of Steven standing in front of a jury, pleading the case of his client. She knew she would never be faced with him in court, for he practised criminal law, and she specialised in family law. She had however heard of Jessica, his fiancée, and hoped one day to be able to chat with her about her practise. Anna and Joseph downstairs were like parents to them all, and Greg, well, she had seen he only had eyes for Suzie at the party. He was going to be a pleasure to get to know, especially as he was a baker. Isabella couldn't resist the smells that emanated upwards from his sessions in the kitchen.

It was cold outside, the fourth of December, and although the sky was blue, it was one of those crisp days where scarves were needed. The North Face coat that she had treated herself to last winter was keeping out the bitter wind. Its tiny wisps biting into her exposed face reminded her to buy some more moisturiser; this cold was playing havoc with her skin.

As she hailed a taxi, its inviting warmth was a delight to behold.

"Covent Garden," she instructed the driver and then sat back and watched as the sights of London went by. A double-decker bus, red as a freshly picked rose, gliding along the bus lane, carrying its passengers to God knows where. The teachers on their way to school, the waitresses knowing they were going to have to smile all day, even if they didn't feel like it. So many people jostling for their position in the world, ever moving and evolving to be bigger and better. Isabella knew in her heart that things would never be the same again, but she had to keep everything together for the children and for her own sanity.

Crichton's was in full swing when she arrived, photographers snapping away at what seemed like an endless line of much-too-pretty men and women. Isabella knew how hard it was to stay in shape, but these youngsters made no effort. They had youth on their side, and once dressed by Suzie, they took on a whole new identity. Wasn't that Chloe Mallery? Isabella had seen her in a big ad campaign that Suzie had run last year; she was absolutely flawless. If not for the sullen look between takes, Isabella would have assumed she was beautiful inside and out. She found herself wondering what made this beautiful girl so very sad when, to all on the outside, she had it all: a fabulous career, beautiful clothes, shoes to die for and men falling at her feet. Isabella was sure she would never find out this girl's story but something inside her told her differently. She knew this face, but not from the billboards. No, it was from somewhere else.

Suzie was sitting in her beloved chair, a tapestry wingback that she had found for a bargain price of £12 in a little flea market in Greenwich. She loved nothing more than sourcing furniture that made her happy. After all, she spent many hours in her compact little studio, so it had to be just perfect. Rising to her feet as she saw Isabella approach, she stretched out her arms and embraced the woman with a gigantic hug. To both their surprise, they both needed that hug in more ways than one.

"How are you, Suzie?" Isabella said as she released her new friend and took one of the smaller chairs on the other side of the table. It was a lovely space filled with beautiful designs, and she felt at ease completely. Smiling a little as the design for the dress she had picked out that very day adorned the wall opposite the big window that looked right out into the market square. Its turquoise and pastel greens made a lovely statement on this cold winter's day.

"You look stunning" Suzie mused as she laughed a little, "even if I do say so myself." The friends shared a little moment of appreciation of each other, one as the designer and the other as the perfect model for the creation. Yin and Yang, Isabella had called it when she first tried on the stunning dress. Crichton's had a new client, and Isabella was going to flaunt these designs all over London.

"So, where do we go from here?" Suzie posed the question. She knew the answer; she just wanted Max gone. No big fight, no "he said this she said that," just a clean split. She was offering to buy Max out of the apartment, and he had no rights over her business. She had insisted he sign a prenuptial agreement before she married him to protect her beloved Crichton's and all that it stood for. After all, it was her hard work, blood, sweat and tears that had turned it into the business that she saw before her today.

"Max has agreed to it all," Isabella said with a hint of disappointment in her voice. "I was hoping for a bit of a fight," she said with a huge smile on her face. "Makes my job a little more exciting," she said as Suzie rose to her feet and started her usual stride back and forth. It was finally going to be over — her short-lived marriage and ties to Max. Whatever the future held, she knew that he was never going to be part of it again.

"Let's go and celebrate over some lunch in the market," Suzie said as she grabbed her coat and her beloved Mulberry bag. She had become quite attached to it since she and Greg had found it in a second-hand store just off the Marylebone Road, a steal at £40. It retailed at £460 "Shhhh" she said to Greg as she headed for the counter. Her cash exchanging hands so fast she thought the shop assistant might read her mind and know that he was letting that go far too cheaply.

As she held the door open, Isabella knew that the time had come for her to tell her friend everything that was going on with Robert. It wasn't going away, and the tabloids had grabbed hold of the story and run with it. Her husband's every move documented, ripped to pieces, and commented about by every sleazy journalist in London. Old flames had come out of hiding, claiming that they had slept with him. One even said she had had his baby twenty-one years ago! Surely that wasn't true. She would know if her husband had another family, wouldn't she?

Sliding her coat back on and entwining her neck in what seemed like a thousand turns of the chunky scarf her darling Amy had bought her a few Christmases ago, she strode out onto the main concourse of the market. Covent Garden was a throng of activity, with the bustling tourists and juggling entertainers in full swing.

"Hope we can get a table," she said at Suzie, who was headed towards an empty little bistro set perched on the pavement outside her favourite Italian. Georgio's was always packed, and it was survival of the fittest to get an outside dining experience. Suzie had her eyes on the prize, and to her delight, she just beat a burly American man who just wasn't quick enough. "

You got this, darling" he drawled, as she slid her bottom onto the oh-so-familiar woven-backed chair. Its little red and white checked tablecloth, held down by two silver clips, swayed gently in the December breeze. Isabella caught up with her and they laughed and laughed, recalling her energetic sprint to the finish line with glee.

Chapter 33

With contracts signed and the workforce in place, Rosenberg's braced themselves for the onslaught of creating a whole new line for the off-the-peg market. Hours of preparation had already gone into making cutting rooms more efficient and allowing space for the various different stages of the make-up of more than one garment to happen at a time. The cost would outweigh the profit if they could create a collection that would adorn all the stores that the Crichton and Cleeve brand inhabited.

Immanuel (Immy) & Esther Katz had been with Joseph and Anna for the past twenty years; what they didn't know about creating a garment wasn't worth knowing. Esther, being the daughter of one of Joseph's oldest friends, he had jumped at the chance of having her by his side Her seamstress skills knew no bounds, and as she set to work teaching and mentoring his young workforce, they soon became proficient and created exclusive hand-made, embroidered and beaded couture to adorn any fancy gathering in London.

She had met Immanuel, a trainee tailor at the time at Rosenberg's, whose skill with a pair of tailoring shears was a sight to see. He could cut a bolt of cloth effortlessly and never wasted a bit of it! Joseph had taken him under his wing as both his parents had passed away; Joseph felt the need to nurture this well-mannered young man and step in as a father figure to him.

They were in charge of the cutting rooms, sewing rooms and the finishing rooms. They commanded a mutual respect from their team and made everyone feel as if they were part of the Rosenberg family. Ever mentoring and nurturing themselves to allow the best from everyone, thus creating an atmosphere like no other.

"We can do this, can't we Lute?" Immanuel said as the last of the bolts of fabric were stored away in the vast caverns that were the basement below the main cutting rooms.

"Course we can," Luther chimed. "With everyone on board, we have it in the bag, Immy." Close friends from their youth, growing up in the bosom of their family, these two men had forged not only a business relationship but a bond that would never be broken. Issy, Lute and Immy as they nicknamed each other were the three musketeers — all for one and one for all!

"Mum, Dad," Isaac called as he stepped through the door of number two Telford Parade Mansions. All thoughts of work a distant memory for now. He was busy taking care of his beloved Lizzie and their two very hungry new boys.

"What are you doing here?" Anna almost scolded him with her words, then turned to see her youngest son standing in the doorway, a baby carrier in one hand and Lizzie close behind with the other.

"Joseph," come quickly they are here, our babies are here!" All thoughts of her son were lost in the ether as she gently picked up Joseph, cooing all the time into his little chubby face. "Oh, be still my heart" Anna said as she dropped tiny little kisses all over his face. "Get ready, Joshua, you are next," she smiled as she looked on adoringly at the new additions to their ever-increasing family.

"We came a bit early so that you could make the most of it, Mum. Ada and the gang are coming by later for dinner, and you know how much she and Marjorie love these two boys!" Anna surely did. They doted on these two new arrivals, and she feared that they would be thoroughly spoiled by the time they were five. She had forgotten the time; they were all due for dinner at seven. Reluctantly handing Joshua back to his mother, she hurried into the kitchen and started to prepare a feast for her children.

When, finally, the huge dining table was fit to bursting, Anna could relax. The girls all rallied around, serving the food and filling up the big wine glasses that were saved for such occasions. Maud, hanging on her father's every word, drank in even the most miniscule of details being discussed around the table about Rosenberg's. *I'm going to work there one day*, she thought to herself. Little did she know that one day it would all belong to her. Albert, in his highchair at the top of the table, played happily with the bread sticks he had been given and was a sight to behold as he chuckled and chatted his way through dinner.

Chapter 34

Chloe Mallery sat waiting at the foot of the enormous steps leading up to Waterloo Station. The flower vendor had one eye on her and anther on the passers-by. *What a great way to make a living*, she thought to herself; nobody else to answer to, just yourself and your lovely customers. As she sat there, she remembered a story her dad had told her about a train robber called Buster Edwards. Was this him? Wow, what if it was a real live train robber selling flowers right where she was?

"Chloe!" he shouted and raised her from her daydreaming. "Come on, or we will be late." As she scooped up her belongings and headed up the steps to where he was standing, Robert Collier stretched out his arms and hugged his daughter to him.

"Hello, Dad," she beamed and kissed his cheek once either side, making a joke of it with an air kiss instead.

"Ha ha, very funny," he said, grabbing hold of her and tickling her ribs as if she were still a carefree girl.

"Stop it, Dad," she squealed. "You know I hate to be tickled." As they strode off arm in arm towards the waiting escalators, their steps falling into time as if there was nobody else in the world but them, Robert Collier knew that this bond that they had was going to be broken, and the fallout from this was going to be devastating for them all.

"Where are we going, anyway? You haven't told me a word."

"Let's just get on the train and I will explain as we travel," he said, leading her as far down the platform as he could muster. He knew when they got the other end, their exit needed to be swift.

As they rode the train, Chloe couldn't help but wonder where on earth they were headed and why all the secrecy? She and Robert had such an open and honest relationship, why would he be keeping all of this under his hat?

Robert was frantic. How was he ever going to explain to Chloe that she had a family, a real family? One that she had craved her whole life. He had always told her that Isabella's children were from a different marriage, so were not related to her. Now that the tabloids had got hold of his whole life history, this was going to be a very messy way for her to find out that he had been lying to her for the past twenty-one years.

As the train pulled into the station, Robert could see that their passage was obstructed with photographers and members of the press. He thought he would have been safe at his mother's house. He assumed nobody knew that she lived in Twickenham. But how did they know he was going there today? Someone in his office must have tipped them off. Chloe didn't get it.

"Dad, what's going on?" she said as they pushed past a large group, all snapping and asking questions at the same time.

"Have you left your wife Bobby?"

"Is this your latest fling?"

The questions came thick and fast, and Robert knew he just had to get Chloe out of there and into the nearest taxi. Once her face hit the press, her world would be turned upside down.

The car ride went by in silence. One look at her father's face told Chloe not to speak. He had a foul temper anyway, so she didn't want to provoke him in a public place. She knew how scolding he could be to her mother, and that was one part of his personality that she really didn't like. She saw so much of herself in him, his need to control every situation and to be the best had obviously been handed down from him. Her mother was an amazingly strong woman whom Robert had never married, but he had always taken responsibility for his daughter and for her welfare.

"Hello, Grandma," Chloe smiled from ear to ear as she hugged her favourite person in the whole world close to her chest.

"You smell lovely, my dear. Is that another freebie from those modelling people?"

146

Winnie, her grandma, had no idea what Chloe actually did, and as much as she tried to explain, she never fully got it.

"Yes, Grandma," she nodded in agreement because it was easier than explaining.

"Robert," she said as she looked at her son with bitterness in her eyes. "So today is the day, is it? You finally have to face the truth." Her anger was apparent in her voice but not hurtful, just reproaching. What Isabella would say after finding out about their betrayal, she didn't want to think about just yet!

"Yes, Mother, today is the day." As he squeezed his mum to him, he knew that this was going to be either the end of his time with his daughter or the beginning of something new. Which way this conversation would swing, he had no idea, but he knew that it had to be done and it had to be done here.

Chapter 35

With the Rosenberg's designs all but finished, Suzie and Greg were planning a trip away. When he had asked her, she felt a little nervous. She hadn't known him that long, and what did she really know about this man? Suzie had been drawn to him from the beginning on that beautiful sunny day in Covent Garden. He had been so easy to talk to, and since then, he had seen her through some really tough times.

His camper van, Ethel, had been lovingly packed to its rafters, and Greg had prepared all the food, and so he said, had the mix tape all sorted. Remembering now, how much they had both laughed as the process of good song, bad song unfolded; one drunken night. Sitting lazily at his feet, eating freshly made cheese straws and sipping Merlot that danced on her tongue with the most sensual and velvety texture. Every now and again, he would bend down and kiss her ever so gently, nibbling her lips, causing her to shudder with the thought of him. His very presence making her feel safe and at home.

"It's going to be fine," Kelly, her assistant, said as she hugged her goodbye and waved them on their way.

"I know it will," she said and made Kelly promise to call her if anything came up. Parade Street was deserted, all but Kelly standing there, waving endlessly as she watched her closest friend head out to what she hoped was going to be a great long weekend. The keys to Suzie's apartment in hand, she was going to enjoy having a little space to herself for her and Grady, her fiancé to just chill and relax. Their studio was getting a little claustrophobic, and they both felt the need to just get away from it all.

Ethel was chugging along, her bright red sides and cream stripes looked sleek and shiny in the February light. The VW sign on the front, Greg had told her, was in pride of place. He had hunted high and low for a replacement; the last one had been stolen, much to his utter annoyance. Every part of this baby, he had told her had been tuned, refined and honed back to its original beauty.

"Where are we going, anyway?" Suzie said as she laid back and made herself comfortable in the big red leather seat.

"It's a surprise," Greg said and smiled the wickedest of smiles, and she couldn't help but chuckle at his expression. "No, honestly, you are going to love it," he said as he threw her a packet of Starburst and added, "Save me the red one!"

As the music played in the background, they chatted endlessly about the collection, his book and what was next for them both.

"Let's make a pact," Suzie said, raising her voice in excitement. "No talk of work when we get where we are going." Greg was nodding and smiling.

"Hell yes," he said. "It's a deal."

Suzie had long since realised where they were going; the road signs gave it away a little, but she kept her tongue and didn't give the surprise away until they got very close.

"Oh wow, the New Forest!" she chimed.

Greg beamed with delight and said, "It's my favourite place in the whole wide world. You can get lost in time here." As they pulled off the road and into the trees, Suzie knew she had made the right decision and settled back to enjoy the stay.

Their pitch was sorted, and the van was unloaded into the little awning Suzie had watched Greg effortlessly pull out and erect. A small bistro table, two chairs, wine by the bottle and two glasses were accompanied by some overly large Tupperware boxes, a small metal drum they later used as a fire pit, and even more Tupperware stored at Greg's feet. A cosy oversized blanket between them, and the second mix tape gently took them back to places in their youth.

As Greg threaded overly sized marshmallows onto damp skewers, Suzie had the feeling that he had done this before. She allowed him to take the lead and just sat back and enjoyed the new experiences. After all, she had never been camping before.

Max had always said, "If I have to drive four hours, just imagine where the plane could take us in that time." She liked this new adventure and all the taste sensations Greg had prepared for them both.

"Dessert first, I love it," Suzie said as she took a bite of the first toasted marshmallow she had ever eaten. Greg couldn't believe she had never done this before.

"This is my very own recipe," he teased, and Suzie was in awe of this amazing man who could make her feel special, whatever he did.

"What do you think?" Greg said, placing a whole marshmallow into his mouth and regretting it once the heat got to work on his tongue. Glugging down nearly half a glass of the cool Sauvignon Blanc, he half choked, half coughed, trying to alleviate the burning sensation at the back of his throat.

Suzie, as quick as a flash, was upon him, patting him on the back and placing the ice she had in her glass into his mouth. The cool sensation eased the pain, allowing Greg to calm a little before kissing her firmly on the mouth. All thoughts of pain melted away as their kiss became more and more intense.

"You make me feel as if electricity is passing through my whole body when you kiss me," Greg whispered into Suzie's ear.

"That's love you are feeling," she said without thinking, "from me to you."

Stopping Greg in his tracks, had she just said the L word to Greg? Oh no, she had, and now she had to go on as if nothing had happened. Greg, ever the gentleman, carried on as usual and just smiled inwardly. This beautiful girl, his beautiful girl, was falling in love with him as he was with her.

Recipe Four — Cheese Straws (Rebel Baker)

100g soft butter
225g plain flour
¼ tsp salt
100g grated cheddar cheese
1 egg yolk
20g parmesan to sprinkle

Method:
Pre-heat oven to 210 °C for a fan oven.
Rub together butter, flour and salt until it resembles breadcrumbs. Mix in the cheese and egg yolk until you have a soft dough.
Roll out the dough into a rectangle measuring 7" x 10" and sprinkle the parmesan over it..
Cut the dough into 24 fingers and twist if desired.
Transfer the cut dough to a lightly greased baking sheet and bake for 8 – 10 minutes until golden brown.
Allow to cool on a rack before serving.

Recipe Five — Marshmallows (Rebel Baker)
50g Cornflour

50g Icing Sugar
50g Liquid Glucose
450g Caster Sugar
10 sheets of gelatine
2 large egg whites
2 vanilla pods
(Optional — food colouring, rose water, orange blossom water, lemon extract, peppermint extract)

Method:

Sieve the cornflour and icing sugar into a bowl, then finely sift half the mixture over a deep baking tray measuring 20 cm x 30cm. Set the remaining mixture aside to dust the top.

Mix the liquid glucose syrup and sugar together in a pan over a low heat with 250ml cold water.

Heat gently and stir until sugar is dissolved and you have a clear syrup. Meanwhile, soak the gelatine sheets in 125ml of water.

Once the sugar syrup is clear, pop a sugar thermometer in the pan and allow the syrup to boil vigorously. Do not stir the syrup. When it reaches 110°C, place the gelatine pan over a medium heat and stir until dissolved.

Whisk the egg whites with an electric mixer until stiff peaks form. When the sugar syrup reaches 122°C very carefully and slowly pour it down the side of the bowl of the moving mixer, then pour in the gelatine.

Halve the vanilla pods lengthways and with the tip of a knife, scrape the seeds out and add to the mixer. Continue mixing for another 6 – 8 minutes or until the mixture has significantly increased in volume but is still thick and pourable.

This is the time to add any colours or flavours, you may want white vanilla or, you can add any of the flavours listed above. Remember to start small and add to taste. Whisk for another couple of minutes, so the colour and flavour is evenly mixed.

Pour the marshmallow mixture into your prepared tray and use an oiled palette knife to smooth it out. Sift over the remaining mixed icing sugar and cornflour and place somewhere to cool for 2 – 3 hours or until set and soft. Use cutters or slice marshmallow into even sized cubes.

Chapter 36

Rosenberg's was in full swing, the vast cutting tables amassed with pattern pieces galore. How on earth they differentiated between them was anyone's guess, but they did it with ease and they did it with style. The green baize was laid out lovingly on each table, a testament to the times of satin fabrics and silks galore. The fuzzy texture stopping the fabric from slipping as it was cut into every shape possible. The new textiles of the day were not so luxurious and far easier to tame. Esther was overseeing everything fabric-related, while Immanuel took control of the final product and packing for release to the Cleeve's distributors.

"Mary, please come in," Luther said as he rose to his feet to welcome their long-awaited visitors. "So lovely to finally meet you in person." Mary beamed as she shook his hand then very gently decided to hug him.

"Sorry, Luther, I am a hugger; you will get used to me." Her Crichton creation designed by Suzie herself, was a take on a Chanel classic but with a twist of sheer brilliance because it was made of taffeta. Everyone knew that when treated right, taffeta was strong and robust and could be cut into any style they desired. It was the colour of sunshine, and other than an old paste brooch that Mary had picked up in Camden Lock, it looked every part as if she had stepped off a catwalk in Paris. Her matching shoes and bag, a gift from a fellow designer, were nothing short of divine excellence. Jordan strode into the room behind her, never overshadowing his wife but looking ever so elegant in his own creation. A houndstooth tweed three-piece suit finely cut with shallow lapels and adorned with a splash of colour from the canary yellow tie and his signature socks, revealed as he took a seat beside his wife. The bright yellow served as a stark reminder to Luther that he really ought to dress better than he did in the office.

"Hello, young man," Jordan's voice gentle and kind, not at all gruff as Luther had imagined it would be. "We have taken the tour and seen everything," he winked at his wife as he spoke.

"It all seems to be running smoothly, and the distributers are waiting with bated breath to see the final garments adorn their rails," Mary spoke with a beautiful diction and an elegance that Luther had never really heard before. His clients may have been wealthy, but Mary Cleeve was a cut above them all. A self-made millionaire, she had no airs or graces; she just oozed elegance and sophistication from every pore. He was going to enjoy working alongside this formidable woman and her oh-so-distinguished husband.

As they secured the last few delivery slots and allowed Immanuel to walk them through the final stages, the boys looked on in awe, watching this beautiful couple smile and coo at each other throughout what can only be described as one of the best meetings in the history of Rosenberg's.

As the door closed behind them, Luther said with the ease of friendship, "Immy, we did it. I knew we could, and we did."

"Yes, Lute, we did it. Wait until we tell Issy; he is going to kick himself that he has missed all this." But of course, Isaac wasn't missing work at all; his two boys were seeing to that.

The door to number two seemed to Anna as a revolving contraption that she had seen in a hotel once, with someone coming or going through its large expanse all hours of the day and night. She caught sight of her fellow Mansion dwellers every now and then. She made a mental note to go and see Greg, who always seemed to be with Suzie and the lovely Stephen, very soon. She wanted to hear all about his engagement to Jessica.

Luther and Immanuel came rushing through the door, chattering so loudly that Anna had to chastise them.

"Shhh," she said as quietly as she could, "You will wake the boys."

"Oh, give over, Mum. The more noise you make, the sounder they will sleep," Luther interjected as she shot him a disapproving gaze.

"You youngsters think you know it all," Anna said as she patted her eldest son on the chest and offered him a cup of coffee.

"Immy, so lovely to see you. How is Esther doing?" Immanuel broke into a sudden rendition of everything that had happened over the last few weeks, and everyone just sat at the big kitchen table, listening on and enjoying the banter between the three grown men. Lizzie every now and again adding a little something to make the boys laugh. As Joseph entered the lively kitchen, both his boys stood up and rushed to him.

"Sit down, Dad. Take the load off your feet," Luther said as he took hold of his dad by the hand and lowered him gently into his seat like an aged old ruin.

"Boys, stop fussing. I am fine. It's your mother you should be taking care of, not me!" All eyes went to Anna,

"Why? What's wrong with Mum?" they all chimed at the same time. Anna laughed so loud she broke the silence, and as she did, the twins in unison started to cry.

"Make as much noise as you like, eh?" Anna said as she strode out of the kitchen and into the beautiful nursery where her grandsons resided. All thoughts of the business long forgotten, she had a new job to do and was loving every minute of it. Joseph, on the other hand, was missing the day-to-day briefings and being involved in his beloved Rosenberg's. *Will my sons forget me completely?* He wondered to himself silently.

Chapter 37

"Steven, how lovely to see you," Anna almost sang the words. She loved Steven and was so excited for his upcoming marriage to Jessica. "It's been a little hectic here, to say the least" she beamed.

"Grandmotherhood suits you," Steven said with a chuckle, which made Anna laugh out loud and hug him to her. "I am just going up to drop my bag off, is that coffee I smell?" he said as he took the stairs two at a time, calling behind him, "See you in a minute." Anna went back inside and busied herself with elevenses, as she and Joseph loved to call them.

The table laid, her cherished china all set out, as she always said everything tastes better from a china cup. Her mama's dowry to her daughter as she set off in her new marriage. Every piece still intact all these years later; how many stories could these cups recite? So many moments to be thankful for. Joseph watched in awe as she pottered about, fussing with linen napkins and just the right-sized plates.

Greg had given them some of his cinnamon buns to try, and these were pride of place as Steven rushed through the door and parked himself in his usual spot just opposite Joseph.

"Hello, my boy, so lovely to see you," Joseph chirped. He missed seeing his own boys every day, so this delightful interlude was much needed. After all, being happy was not just about having a big life; it was about all the moments that made that life good. Steven was straight into the coffee and the buns and didn't stop until half the plateful had been consumed, chattering all the while about Jessica and all their plans for what he hoped would be the best day of their life.

"Joseph, can I ask something of you?" changing the mood from carefree to serious just like that.

"Of course, my boy, what do you need?" Steven wanted a suit but not something that was hired or off the peg. He had dreamed of having a suit made, and who better than Joseph to create this for him.

"Would you make me a wedding suit?" The smile on Josephs face said it all; he missed his work so very badly. Anna could see how sad he had become, and he needed this new commission to keep his mind, body and spirit active.

"Yes, my boy, I would be delighted to accommodate you," the excitement in his voice clear for all to hear. *This is a good day*, he thought to himself and another moment to add to the list.

Steven had been involved in a large criminal trial that had been all over the news and had everyone talking. He couldn't say anything about it, but he was glad that today was an easier day. The jury was out for deliberation, and it could take days. Taking the time to relax a little and concentrate on his lovely Jessica, he was ploughing through a list of jobs that he had been putting off for far too long.

Goodbyes done and a few cinnamon buns for the road, he headed back up to his own apartment. There was much still to do before he met Jessica for dinner that evening. What on earth was she going to say when he told her that he was thinking of taking a sabbatical from the law practice that he worked for and going into a community refuge to help women in domestic violence cases? Steven knew this was a field in which he felt he could succeed. After all, his own Mother had fled with him as a boy to just such a place, so he could empathise with all of them.

That was a productive day, Steven thought to himself as he sped across town in a taxi to meet Jessica. The streets were lined with tourists, and thankfully, he had reserved a table at a little bistro in Covent Garden. He knew full well he would never just get a table if he just rocked up unannounced. Jessica was waiting for him as he stepped out of the taxi. Her lovely face shone as he approached her with a smile that melted her heart. This man truly loved her, and she could see it and hear it in every look and every word. The gentlest of kisses, and they were on their way, stopping every now and again to watch a street entertainer or two.

"What's the matter?" Jessica said as they were seated at their table.

"Wow you are good." She knew him so very well already and could spot his moods at a glance.

"Well, you have been very quiet of late, and it's not just the case you are on," Jessica said with the hint of a puzzled look on her face. She wasn't concerned too much, though, because she knew he would tell her eventually. He always did.

As he explained his plans, Jessica's smile got wider and wider, and to his sheer delight, she was all for it!

"I love it," she said, taking his hands across the table into hers. "When will you start?" As if she had to ask, she knew it was going to be imminent. Why else would he be so agitated?

"Two weeks from today," he said with a hint of a smile, and with that, they both burst out laughing, the tension broken and the love between them apparent.

"Bravo," she said with a little clap of her hands. "Let's eat!"

"Hello, you two." Their moment of jollity broken, they both looked up to see Greg and Suzie standing there, heading towards a nearby table.

"Hey, come and join us," Jessica smiled. "We are celebrating, oh unless, of course, you want to be alone?" As Greg and Suzie looked at each other, both nodding their approval, they signalled to the waiter.

"Could they sit here?" With a flourish of activity, the table was set for four, and their evening began.

Chapter 38

"Come on, then, tell me it all and leave nothing out!" Suzie settled herself in for the night as Isabella recited chapter and verse from the early days of their marriage to the saga that was unfolding every day in the press. She leaves no stone unturned, and in a way, it's so very good to say the words out loud.

Robert, from the start, had been a womaniser; she had no clue about their names or what they did or even where they were from. It didn't matter because she couldn't stop him. He loved himself, and some would say he was a narcissist. He faked empathy to make people like him, and he could charm the birds from the trees if need be. Why did she let him control her? After all, she was successful in her own right, and he could never take the credit for that.

Isabella told Suzie how hard it was for her to live with this very controlling, sex and self-obsessed man. His need for all things to be just so, and for him and his OCD world, that was fine. But he was enforcing his rules and regulations on her and the children too. Surely, he could see how harmful this was to them all?

Isabella loved to give her children the joy of expressing themselves. Whatever they wanted to be, they could be, as far as she was concerned. She could see every time one of them left a jacket on a chair or their shoes in the wrong spot, he would bristle with fury, managing to keep it in check most of the time, facing his own demons to control the urge to just bark orders and be heard. His rules for three-minute showers and what they could and couldn't have on their feet in each room were debilitating, to say the least. Most of the time, they chose to walk barefoot because it was easier than the constant changing of footwear. Although having to wash one's feet before standing on the plush white carpet that he had insisted be fitted in the upstairs rooms in their first family home was a stretch too far for all of them.

"Mummy I can't do this," Ava could be heard saying over and over again. "My hair is too long to get cleaned in three minutes." Isabella, knowing this was both her girls' problems, would try and make a joke of it, saying that they should shower once Daddy wasn't there. As for the feet cleaning, this became a joke to them too — how many steps in bare feet they could take to get what they needed and not leave a mark. Saying it out loud now made Isabella realise that she was to blame for this. She had allowed Robert to do this to them all. Well, never again. She was done, and he was never stepping foot in that apartment again, whatever he had on his feet!

"So let me get this straight, Amy didn't come home and stay because of the rules her dad was placing on you all?"

"Yes," Isabella nodded, finally being able to say the words. He was driving his children away, and if she let him continue, they would be gone, and she would be left with nobody. After all, Robert was so busy cheating; she couldn't imagine him staying forever, and nor did she want him to.

He spent endless hours on the telephone. His obsession with sex had taken over his life, and he craved it daily. Demanding her whenever he wanted, and when not at home, getting his fix wherever it suited him. Never a thought to how that made Isabella feel, and in hindsight, she felt pretty useless, really. Even though she had sex with her husband usually twice a day, she wasn't enough and never would be. Oh, he had tried counselling but refused to go after just a few months.

"It's a waste of time," he said on more than one occasion, "there is nothing wrong with me!"

Suzie listened with interest and a sense of bewilderment. How had Isabella kept all this to herself for such a long time? It was right what they say — you never know what goes on behind closed doors.

"I don't think you should manage your own divorce," Suzie said with certainty in her voice.

"But that's what I do!" Isabella knew as soon as she had said it that her friend was right. She couldn't do this; she was not thinking straight. This needed to be handled right and with the best outcomes for her and the children. She knew exactly who she was going to approach. Why had she not thought of it sooner? Jessica Edwards. She was renowned in her field to be great at her job, always putting herself out for her clients and getting the best possible outcomes for the families involved. As Isabella shared her thoughts with Suzie, the smile that crept across her face told her the answer before she even said it.

"Yes, yes and yes, she is the perfect choice."

As the Shiraz flowed and the food came and went, Suzie felt relaxed in her new friends' company. They had a bond after all. They loved clothes and both their husbands were cheaters. As Suzie raised her glass for a toast, she laughed so loudly that the young couple on their romantic date beside them both looked on in wonder.

"To cheating husbands!" she resounded, the statement loud for all to hear. How many that night were sitting with their mistresses or misters, for that matter, she didn't know or care. Tonight was about helping her friend get back the life that she knew she deserved. As they laughed and laughed, Isabella knew that whatever Robert's secrets, she could face them with her friends at her side.

"Waiter, could we have the bill please?" Suzie her hand in the air, frantically fuelled by the glorious red wine she had consumed far too much of.

"No dessert ladies?" came his resounding reply.

"Oh no, thank you I have the perfect solution for a final course." Winking at the waiter Suzie didn't need to say anything more. As they gathered their coats and said their goodbyes, there was only one place that Suzie wanted to be, and that was sat at Greg's kitchen table with a slice of his delicious chocolate cake in front of her.

Chapter 39

The night air hit them both full in the face as they swayed to keep upright. Isabella clung onto Suzie's arm for her life.

"Ooh stop the world, I want to get off!" she yelled at the top of her voice. Suzie, knowing full well that a London taxi driver would never let them both travel in this state, tried to steady her friend enough to avoid the swaying. Once hailed, Isabella stowed away in the back seat, and they were on their way. Suzie could see the driver looking in his rear-view mirror; he wasn't going to throw them out now, not two women on their own. She smiled sweetly and mouthed "thank you" to appease the annoyance in his eyes. Isabella put her head on her friend's shoulder and drifted off into a motionless sleep, looking at peace for once that day, as if she didn't have a care in the world.

As they glided along the streets, so familiar to Suzie, at this point in her life, she couldn't see herself living anywhere else in the world. Yes, she had dreamed of big houses full of children in the countryside, but this was her home, her roots were here, and in some way, she knew in her heart that it would be the hardest decision in her life to ever move away.

Having pre-warned Greg of their imminent arrival, he was standing in his window as the taxi drew up outside the Mansion House. Paying the driver and giving him a rather large tip, Suzie scooped her friend out of the back of the car and steered her towards the big doors, where Greg was now waiting to escort them to their homes.

Isabella safely ensconced in her apartment, Suzie having removed her coat and her shoes, laid her on her big sprawling bed, covered her in a blanket and kissed her gently on the forehead.

"It's all going to be okay," she whispered for nobody really to hear. Filling a large glass with water and adding a couple of paracetamol she found on the nightstand, Suzie took one last look at her friend and headed for the lift. Isabella was going to need them, of that she was certain.

Downstairs, Greg was busying himself picking up discarded balls of crumpled paper. Having printed a chapter or two, he just couldn't get it how he wanted it. His glasses still sitting on top of his ebony curls, the five o'clock shadow looking more like midnight, he found himself smiling because he missed her and he needed her in his arms. He craved the smell of her, the taste of her, and the very presence of her. Now *why can't I just write that in my book*,, he thought to himself? Chastising his own words in his head, Greg knew he didn't want a

"Mills & Boon"; he wanted real-life romance. He needed to put into words exactly how he felt about Suzie.

Tapping gently on the door, Suzie tiptoed in, trying not to make a song and dance of it. After all, it was late, and the Rosenbergs would be sleeping; the slumber of the old filled with dreams of bygone days and wishes fulfilled.

Greg strode across the room and almost engulfed her in his arms. He needed to touch this precious woman who was consuming his thoughts and tormenting his senses. The aroma of perfume and wine fought with each other for first place. Planting a kiss on her mouth, she yielded to him, and they stood there in silence for what seemed like an eternity. His chest so firm beneath her head it felt as if it were made of iron. Words were not needed, just this sensual and all-encompassing embrace.

"Have you got any cake?" Suzie laughed as she said it, batted her eyelids at Greg, and stuck out her bottom lip.

"You only want me for my baking skills," he said squeezing her one last time before having to let her go. "Well, you are in luck," he said, "because I am having a terrible time formulating my last couple of chapters and have been baking on and off for a few days."

As she slid herself into what was now her seat at the table, Suzie smiled the biggest smile Greg had ever seen.

"You know what?" she said. "This feels like coming home!"

As Greg edged the cake towards her, sitting himself as close as he could, he whispered "this is like no home I have ever felt, and I love it!"

Chapter 40

His mother's house in Twickenham seemed a far cry from his beautiful penthouse apartment. The shabby interior showed its age. Winnie, his mother, hadn't let him touch a thing when her beloved Robert had passed away.

"Leave it be," she had said to her son every time he came and wanted to update this or knock down that. "Do what you want with it when I am dead, my boy. It's all yours anyway, but until that day, it remains as your father left it."

As Chloe came back into the sitting room, clutching a steaming mug of tea and a few biscuits (she needed carbs today!), her dad and grandma were both standing at the old wooden bar. Her dad had a large glass of red wine in his hand, her grandma had a bitter lemon in hers. Her grandpa had loved to serve drinks from behind there every party they had. She missed those carefree days of growing up in this beautiful house; she and her mum had moved in when she was born.

"Grandpa always loved that bar," she said to nobody in particular, and they all raised their drinks in a cheers. Tears pricked Winnie's eyes as she remembered just how lonely she was without Robert.

They had met when they were just teenagers, and everyone had said that it wouldn't last. Well, they showed them. Forty-two years and they would still have been going strong if that awful stroke hadn't gripped Robert to the point where he couldn't speak or walk. In some ways, the second stroke a few weeks later was a blessing in disguise.

Robert had always said, "If anything ever happens to me and I can't communicate, then switch me off." He would have hated what he had become. So, when the phone call came that day to say that her brave Robert had passed away in his sleep, she knew that he was in a far better place.

"Come on, Dad," Chloe broke the silence between them. "What on earth are we doing here? Why all the photographers and the secrecy?" She had so many questions, but she knew he had to tell her in his own time and in his own way.

"Chloe, you know that I love you and that I loved your Mum very much?"

"Yes, Dad, you told us that every single day when I was growing up."

"Well, I have kept something from you, and I know now that it was wrong of me to do so. I should have told you at the start, but I didn't know how to. So, my darling girl, I have written you a letter because there is far too

173

much to tell, and I want you to remember it all, not just snippets of a conversation."

With that, Robert, envelope in hand, strode across the room, slung his arms around *his Chloe* as he always called her, and placed the smooth creamy paper between her fingers. Its warmth overwhelmed her senses as it had been in his inside pocket, tucked away from prying eyes. Chloe turned on her heels, and without hesitation, headed for the hallway, up the stairs and into what was her childhood bedroom.

She hadn't been in this room since leaving home at eighteen. Her grandpa had helped her to pack all her belongings that she needed for her new digs, as he had called them, at university. Elizabeth, her mother, had been busy that weekend moving herself into Peter's little Victorian house situated right by Twickenham rugby ground. They were both leaving for new adventures, and Chloe was happy for her Mum. She had given up so much to take care of her — the ballet lessons and extra tuition to help with her studies. Nothing was ever too much for her beautiful Clo Clo, as she had always lovingly called her. As for Peter, she couldn't remember a time when he wasn't there. Always patient and on the sidelines, waiting for the day that Elizabeth would finally be his.

The room hadn't changed at all, from the posters on the walls to the flowery pink curtains that hung at the window. Wow, this was a step back in time; her first kiss had happened right there on that bed. Billy Baxter, his name was, and he had big front teeth. Chloe found herself smiling at the thought of him. She wondered what he might be doing now. Propping up the pastel pink pillows, she nestled herself against the headboard and settled down to read. Her stomach was in knots, for she knew things may never be the same again.

Darling Chloe,

Where, oh where, to begin. I suppose at the beginning, but for this I have to go further back than when you were born.

In the summer of 1990, I met and was dating Isabella, my now wife. She was an aspiring lawyer, and I was in total awe of her. Back then, as now, I had no idea how to treat a lady. It meant nothing to me to court Isabella and date other women behind her back. Little did I know that this behaviour would lead me to where I am right now! Homeless and very much alone.

We had such fun, and she is, without a shadow of a doubt in my mind, my soulmate. "Right," I hear you saying, "there is no such thing Dad." Well, let me tell you that the mere sight of her makes my knees wobble, and I drown in the scent and absolute beauty of her. But me being me, I have blown it royally.

Whilst I was dating Isabella, I worked on a very large project in London — late nights on the building site, long weekends away from home and my need never to be alone brought me to the arms of your mother, Elizabeth Mallery. She was a project coordinator, and we spent many hours locked away together where, of course, the inevitable happened. I spent half the week with Isabella and half the week living with Elizabeth. Neither knew about the other. No mean feat on my part, I had code words for the home I was going to; Isabella was 16 and Elizabeth was 29 — the numbers of the front doors of their homes. I used to say to Elizabeth, "I am leaving 16 now and will be at 29" at whatever time it would be. Number 16, in her head, was a grotty little bedsit that I had rented from a colleague at work. In reality, it was a three-bedroom home that I had purchased with Isabella for us to start a family in.

When our first daughter, Amy was born, we were both over the moon. I was still splitting my time between the two houses, and to all intents and purposes, it was working out really well. When Elizabeth told me that she was expecting our baby, my world was turned upside down. What on earth was I going to do, and how was I going to explain this? I sat your mother down in your grandma's kitchen and I told her everything. She was beyond furious and told me that she never wanted to see me again. She and I both knew, though, that she couldn't afford a baby on her salary and on that very day a pact was made between us. She and you, when you were born, would both move into the house at Twickenham. She wanted nothing more to do with me, but would not stop me from seeing you, and agreed that you needed your grandparents.

So, Isabella, to this day, still has no notion that you even exist. For you, my darling, I have always told you that Isabella's children are from another marriage; well, I lied, each and every one of them is mine. We have Amy, of course, Harry, Lilly and Ava. They know nothing of their stepsister as you know nothing of them.

When Isabella and I found out seven years ago that Ava was on the way, we decided that we liked life as it was, and up until that point, had never married. When your grandpa died, it was decided that we should marry so that the children, if anything happened to me, would be safe, Isabella too. So, by telling you that Isabella really didn't want anything to do with you over the years and not allowing you to come to the wedding, I have literally deceived everyone, for nobody knows about my families.

When the tabloids saw me again in the arms of another young woman, this time digging deeper to find out more, little did I know that your mother had spoken to a journalist and told them all about you. She even gave them an old picture of you that was printed in a magazine. So far, nobody has twigged that Elizabeth Mallery is, in fact, Chloe Mallery's mother. For what I know will happen once this explodes, I can only tell you how truly sorry I am.

My next step is to talk to Isabella, as I owe her an explanation, and to my children, who need to know they have a stepsister.

So, from the bottom of my heart, I ask for forgiveness. I ask you to allow me to try and sort this all out and I pray to God every day that my beloved Isabella and all of my five children won't be destroyed because of me.

Always yours, Dad xx

As Chloe folded the letter and placed it back into its envelope, her name beautifully written on the front, she knew that she had to get out of that house and as far away from the people in it as she could.

Collecting up her belongings, she tiptoed down the stairs, picked up her coat and left without looking back. Never again would she step foot inside the home she had loved to live in as a child. Her grandma and dad were so engrossed in their conversation they hadn't even noticed that she had gone. They had all betrayed her, and she had no concept of forgiveness in her heart. Robert Collier was going to be a very lonely old man, she thought to herself.

Chapter 41

Laura was due at a script meeting first thing in the morning. David Summers was going to be there, and she'd really had enough of him and his demands of her. She needed to clear her head, to think, to decide. She had done so much wrong to so many people. How could one night with Nick make her see all of that? He was the kindest, gentlest man, just like the boy she remembered. At school, they had been inseparable; he was always there to fetch and carry, get her lunch, walk her home — the list was endless. How had she not seen all the qualities that he possessed? She hurt him so much just by being herself! At college, she used him, only when she wanted something and discarded him for other boys that caught her eye. After all, she was Laura Nelson; the queue of boys wanting her was endless.

Her flat felt empty. Nick had gone back to his house in Hammersmith. Laura knew that he lived there because she had seen a spread in Hello! magazine showing Nick Cole in his new home. She remembered thinking at the time what fabulous taste he had in furniture, and wow, what a house. As she busied herself tidying up and arranging her clothes for the next day, her thoughts were all of him. How had she let this gorgeous, kind and generous man get away?

The studios were situated on the South Bank, a favourite place for Laura as she loved to walk alongside the Thames. It brought her such peace in her hectic life. Being part of a TV show had been a dream of hers for so long. Now that she was actually living that dream, its reality was all-encompassing. It was all there was — endless rehearsals, script learning and being pushed and pulled all day to be the person David Summers needed her to be, both on-screen and off. With her head held high, Laura Nelson strode into the studio for what was probably going to be the last time. What on earth was she thinking trying to be somebody else, when all she ever wanted to be was herself? Lauryl Simmonds, who was she?

"Hello, darling," Judy, the production assistant, hugged Laura tightly to her. They had been friends from the start. Thirty years Laura's senior, she had been around the block a few times over the years and had chewed up and spat out better than David Summers.

"Keep away from him" she had pleaded with Laura on many occasions. Judy could see right through Lauryl Simmonds; she was a hard nut to crack, but beneath that hard exterior was the real woman she knew that she could be. "If you let him treat you like that, they all will darling girl." Laura knew she was right and tried so very hard to get away from him. Not realising that if she just said no, he couldn't do anything to her. She had a contract, and the studio bosses loved her. She ticked every one of the boxes that they had asked David to fulfil.

With a new steely expression fixed firmly on her face, keeping the vision of Nick in her mind, she pushed open the door to the production office, sat herself down, and showed everyone just what she was capable of. Taking charge of the meeting, getting involved in decisions about the script, the set, and even the order with which they would shoot the scenes. She was no longer going to sit back and let David Summers control her. The next few hours went so quickly she could hardly believe it. As the final "any other business" was asked, the meeting came to a close. As Laura stood up, David Summers grabbed her hand,

"Sit back down," he demanded. From the depths of her very being, Laura faced him.

The room still full to bursting, she said for all to hear, "Take your hands off me, and if you ever touch me again, you will regret ever knowing me." And with a look of anger and disbelief, David Summers took to his feet.

"You are nothing without me, Lauryl Simmonds, and don't you forget it. I was good enough when you needed to climb the ladder." He was right. Laura had used him, but not any more. She was turning a new page and starting a new chapter.

"The name is Laura Nelson," she beamed, "and don't you forget it, you pathetic excuse for a man!"

The applause could be heard down the corridor as David Summers retrieved his coat and headed out into the cool light of day.

"Bravo!" were the cheers from so many of the female members of staff, and even some of the older, more established men took to their feet and bowed to her with grace. As she dialled his number, she knew that this was a new beginning and hoped that he would join her on this exciting adventure. Being Laura Nelson wasn't that bad after all!

Chapter 42

"Come on, Issy. We are going to be late." Luther, banging on the door of his brother's house, was so impatient. Did he not remember what it was like to have a new baby, let alone two of them?

"Okay, okay, I am coming!" As Isaac kissed his two boys gently on their foreheads, his heart swelled with love for them. Lizzie was standing at the door, his bag in hand. Smiling, she raised her head to kiss him gently on the lips, knowing that everything was going to be just fine. Her man was heading back to work, her mama was just around the corner and she had this.

"Bye-bye my girl. See you later," he said as he walked down the drive towards Luther's waiting car. They needed a little prayer to help them all move forward into this new era, he said to himself.

"They will be okay, won't they Lute?" His question falling on deaf ears as Luther had the radio up so very loud. Isaac wondered how his brother coped with the noise.

"I love this song," he said, jigging about a little in his seat. He's supposed to be the sensible one, Isaac thought to himself, and his smile told his brother all he needed to know as he turned the volume up even higher.

Rosenberg's was just as he had left it a few weeks ago, except it was moving at three times its usual pace.

"Blimey, Lute, I had no idea how fast this had all moved on." His expression worried Luther.

"This is it, little brother, this is the big time." He knew, as he said those words, that Rosenberg's was heading in a very different direction than the one that his dad and his brother had envisaged, but he was forging forward with them or without them. He knew that Issy would stay along for the ride, and in some ways, he wished his dad were there too. This was his company, and he needed to see how far it had come.

Esther and Immanuel filled Isaac in on everything that had already taken place. The garments were heading for the finishing rooms, and everyone was so very pleased with the designs. Suzie had excelled. After all, she had Mary and Jordan Cleeve to make an impression on. Her reputation and theirs were on the line. Luther had promised garments fit for a king but affordable to everyone. Nothing had been spared, and so long as everything went to plan, Rosenberg's was going to be a name not only in London, but Paris and New York.

Anna and Joseph were making a rare visit to their once beloved Rosenberg's. The hectic schedule was no longer a worry for them they sauntered through the oh-so-familiar streets, stopping for coffee at their old friend

Ike's café. He had been in business for as long as they had, and his café was the place to go for the best coffee on the planet. Well, that's at least what Anna said every time they went there. Sitting at their usual table, their friend took his seat as he always did, beside Joseph. They chatted about everything as if they had only seen each other yesterday, the ease of real friendships forged over time. It didn't matter how often you saw people; it picked up as if there had never been a gap.

Ike listened to all the stories about the babies and the boys, but not a mention of Rosenberg's. Joseph was too frightened lately to speak of the place, for fear that Anna would know how dreadfully he missed it all. Silly man, thinking that his wife didn't already know his thoughts. She read him like a book, open only for her to see.

As they sat and chatted, to Joseph's surprise, Lute, Issy and Immy came bounding through the door like the boys they used to be. Their banter making each of them laugh and smile, bringing a tear to Anna's eye. Pulling another table over, Ike pushed them together and laid a fresh cloth over both. Food and drink were ordered, and they settled into a steady stream of conversation. Joseph's expression was of sheer delight. He was back in the thick of it all, and it was plain for all to see that it was just where he needed to be.

"Dad, what do you think about coming back and helping out?" Luther spoke with authority; he wasn't joking. He missed his dad and the input of wisdom he had to share with them all. Immanuel and Isaac both nodded in unison, could think of nothing better to happen. Joseph searched Anna's face and saw immediately that she was fine with it.

"My darling Joseph, of course, you must go back. This sabbatical of yours has been fabulous for us both, but you are not cut out to sit at home every day." With a wink to her boys, Anna smiled inwardly. Her job done; Joseph was back where he belonged, and she had two blessed boys to help raise.

Chapter 43

"Are you okay?" Isabella asked her friend as they waited outside the judge's chambers to be let in.

"Yes, all good, I promise," Suzie said, just wanting today to be over and done with so that she could move on with her life and know that she never had to see Max Brompton ever again. After all, she hadn't set eyes on him since her gala dinner and that fateful night when he showed the world exactly what sort of man he was.

"Come on, Holly darling," she heard his voice before she saw him. Walking hand in hand towards Suzie, there they were, but what was she seeing? Holly was pregnant. Max had always said that he didn't want to be a dad and here he was fussing over her like an old mother hen. The tears pricked her eyes as she remembered his words telling her that he never wanted a family, and she had felt so very alone.

"Well, that's a turn-up for the books," Isabella said as she eyed Holly with distain.

Sitting around the big wooden table, Suzie found herself looking at Max. He looked drawn and older. Becoming a father obviously didn't agree with him. His once sharp appearance had been turned into an unshaven, jean-wearing, sweater-hugging older man. Yikes, he was a far cry from Greg; Suzie found herself smiling broadly at the thought of him. They were so very different, and she was falling in love with him. Greg had said he would come today, but Suzie had declined the offer, telling him that she needed to do this alone. Inside, she wanted him there, but she didn't want to seem needy. Holly sat there the whole time like the cat that got the cream. The secretary had hooked the boss and was milking him for all he was worth, by the looks of her expensive maternity wear.

After endless back-and-forth arguments about the apartment, their cars, and the flat Max owned in the city, they came to an agreement. Holly assumed she would be moving into the Mansion apartment, but Suzie was having none of it.

"You are not involved in my divorce," she almost shouted as Holly began to tell the judge that they needed the space for the baby. Suzie had no intention of giving up her home to the woman that her husband had cheated on her with.

Max got to keep his flat, Suzie was to take over the full payments on the Mansion apartment, and they kept their own cars. It was simple, really. No talk of the business, as this was Suzie's, and he had no rights to it, as she had no rights to his practice; a pre-nuptial had sorted that out right back at the beginning.

Formalities over, Max and Holly walked out of the door, and Suzie knew that it was over. As she and

Isabella headed for the foyer, there he was, waiting for her, a bunch of freesias in his hand. Greg had come to support her and make sure she was okay.

As her friend slipped away, knowing that she wasn't needed tonight, Greg took Suzie into his arms and ever so quietly whispered into her ear, "I love you".

Chapter 44

The foyer was filled with much laughter as Isabella, Suzie and Jessica got ready to head into town for a girls' night out.

"Some business first, then the night can begin," Jessica said as she pulled on her boots, still in her hand, as she ran down the stairs. Her jolly snowman socks, a gift from her nephew last Christmas, reminded them all that it wasn't all about glamour. Anna popped her head out of her front door to see what all the commotion was about.

"Hello, girls," she beamed. "So lovely to see you all." They all wished her well and promised to come and see her and Joseph very soon.

"Can we all come together?" Isabella pleaded. "We have so much to tell you both."

"Yes, of course you can. Let's make a date for Sunday lunch next week, if you are all free?"

"Can't wait," their collective response was met by the biggest smile they had ever seen on Anna's face.

"It's a date. We will look forward to it." As Anna went back inside, she could hear Suzie and chuckled to herself.

"Oh my goodness, you didn't use the lift. I love the lift," she said as she looked at it dreamily, not really expanding on her reasons, just letting them know.

"I thought the stairs would be quicker, and I agree that lift is like a time machine, so full of adventure and memories." With the sounds of music coming from Anna's, they headed out into the night. Each of them had a reason to be there but were brought together by one common element: they were all friends.

They had chosen Chinatown as their destination, and Wong Kei's for food. Isabella laughed and laughed about the time she and Robert had gone there for a meal with friends, and he had got so drunk he head-planted into his dinner just as it arrived at the table. Her good friend Simon luckily was with them that night, and he helped her get him home as she knew she wouldn't have the strength to hold him up. Smiling at the thought of her old friend, she made a mental note to call him tomorrow. It had been too long!

The place was buzzing, and they all loved the simplicity of it all. The Formica tables and having to share with strangers made it all the more appealing; you really never knew who you would end up with.

On her second glass of wine, Jessica finally built up the courage to ask Suzie her favour. After all, that is why they were all there.

"Would you mind awfully making my wedding gown?" she blurted out as she helped herself to some sesame prawn toast. *This really will have to stop*, she

191

thought to herself, if she wanted to look half decent in her dress.

"I thought you would never ask," Suzie said, her smile beaming across her face. "Of course, I will. It would be an honour." Jessica all but cried as she jumped out of her seat and ran around the table to hug her friend. As she put her arms around her shoulders, Suzie, unable to stand, just accepted the embrace as if it were the most natural thing in the world. Her new friends meant so much to her. She would do anything for them.

Jessica, returning to her seat, was next in line for the favour. As Isabella plucked up the courage to talk, Jessica could see that she was struggling.

"Let me help you out, Isabella. After all I have seen in the press and the endless gossiping in the rags, can I assume you need a good lawyer?"

Isabella, her mouth wide open, finally grinned and said, "You're good, I didn't even have to say a word."

"Good, I'm better than good." They all laughed, and Jessica, bringing the tone back to serious just for a minute, assured her friend that she would do everything in her power to ensure that both Isabella and the children were well taken care of.

"So," the two women chimed in unison. "What can we do for you Suzie?"

As Suzie looked from one to the other, she giggled and said, "Isabella, you have already done more than enough. I do not know how I will ever repay you."

"Oh, I don't know about that," Isabella chimed. "There are still a few designs not hanging in my wardrobe!" She raised her glass and clinked it with Suzie's, knowing that the deal was done.

"As for you Jessica, honestly there is nothing I want or need. Well, except some advice from both of you, maybe." Looking intrigued, they were both waiting for the questions. Suzie, her smile so wide it showed all over her face said, "I think I might have fallen in love!"

"What?" came the cries of both her friends, and all the people on their table started to stare. The couple at the very end had been so intent on their quiet chattering they literally sighed as the gentle chatter about them rose to a crescendo of laughter, amazement and joy. With all attention piqued across the table, Suzie now wanted the ground to open up and swallow her.

"Thanks, ladies, for that," and as she turned to the rest of the table she said, "nothing to see, no news here," and began to laugh so hard she thought her sides would split.

As she regaled her story of the courthouse foyer, Greg telling her he loved her, she spared them the details of the rest of the conversation because it was way too personal to share. Telling them how he took her out for lunch that day and he was forever the gentleman. Pulling her chair out for her to be seated, taking charge of the wine, and just cooing over her, making sure she had everything that she needed. Her heart fit to bursting, was she mad, had she lost gain of her senses? Suzie knew one thing for sure, she couldn't imagine a life without him. Her friends were thrilled, and they offered her one piece of advice. Follow your heart, Suzie Crichton, for it will lead you where you need to be right now.

"Now, let's get on with this fabulous dining experience and head over to De Hems for a couple or three." Suzie, knowing that there was more than enough time to make decisions, followed her friends' lead. Tonight was supposed to be fun, and fun it was going to be.

De Hems was rocking when they got there. The three of them pushed a path to the bar and luckily had no resistance from the throng of what seemed like an endless stream of twenty-something lads all intent on seeing who could drink their beers the fastest. *A stag night,* Suzie thought to herself, *this is going to get messy later.*

"Hey, ladies" one of the group shouted, "these are on us."

As Isabella leaned in to remove her wine glass from the bar, an overzealous stag said "Hello, beautiful, fancy a dance?" Isabella, ever the lady, turned to 'Pissy Pete'. she knew this was his name as it was printed on his T-shirt.

"Pete, is it? Or do you prefer Pissy?" she said with an air of annoyance. "Look, we are just here to have a drink. At this point in time, we hate men, well, except her," she said, pointing to Jessica. Looking over at

Suzie, who looked stunning in one of Mary Cleeve's creations, she said, "She just got divorced, and I am about to. So, do us a favour and fuck off!"

With that, there was an almighty cheer from the crowd, and Pete's bright red face lit up the room. Laughing, the ladies perched themselves on the bar stools that seemed to have been left unattended like a straight man in a gay bar and got back to their evening.

"Bloody hell, Isabella," Suzie chuckled. "That's one way of getting rid of unwanted attention. Silly boys, all of them. I am sick of men!"

Chapter 45

Having said his goodbyes for now to his colleagues, Steven prepared himself for his new role. He was helping out for six months at a refuge for women in distress. At least he thought that was what they were. What did you call a lady whose husband beat her, or abused her in some way? Not only husbands but boyfriends, fathers, brothers, mothers — the list was endless. He had complete empathy for these ladies and for their children. He himself had been an abused child; his mother and he had so much to thank the refuge for, as they had helped them. It was his turn to give something back.

Brought up on a council estate in the East End of London, Steven knew the hardships of a London life. Street raking from an early age, trying to find odd jobs to help out the family, washing cars, cleaning windows for the local pensioners, and trying his best to help his mum as much as he could. Katie Sandgate was a grafter, salt of the earth, her neighbours called her. His dad, on the other hand, was a good-for-nothing waste of space. He thought nothing of spending his wife's hard-earned money on cigarettes and his gambling addiction, causing Katie to have to take on more shifts at the pub where she worked, and her two cleaning jobs were wearing her out.

Jim Sandgate liked nothing more than barking his orders and literally scaring the life out of his wife and child. They tiptoed around him on eggshells, never really knowing what sort of a mood he would be in from one minute to the next. If he won on the horses, it was all sweetness and light and ice cream after tea. If he lost, he took his frustrations out on his beloved mum. She shielded her only son so many times from harm's way that Steven vowed he would punch him in the face one day.

"There, there, my boy," his mum soothed him one night at bedtime.

"I hate him, Mum. If I was bigger, I would hit him back for you," he looked deep into his mum's eyes, and she knew he meant it. Her precious boy was growing up, and he wouldn't stand for this much longer. What were they to do, and where could they go to escape this toil and torment? Katie plotted every night what she would do. But there she was every morning, still in the same boat.

It was a warm spring day. Steven remembers because he had his shorts on and just a T-shirt. Little did he know that those clothes were the last ones he was ever going to see from his little collection of belongings his mum lovingly washed and ironed week in, week out. He was growing out of everything, and not much else fitted him. As he turned the corner onto Mile End Road, he could see the estate where he lived rising out of the ground. *How many families*, he thought to himself, *were in the same situation, and why didn't anyone help them?* Could they not just go away and live somewhere else, why did they have to live with him?

Katie Sandgate had busied herself in the pub that day, chatting to the regulars and just making do. The local copper had come in a few times and noticed that Katie's eyes were black, and she was looking more and more frail for such a young woman. He had asked her in the past if she needed help, and she always had an excuse-walking into doors or tripping over when her limp was so bad she could hardly stand. Passing her a slip of paper, he shook his head, letting her know not to read it now. She slipped it into her pocket and smiled at him, her thanks clearly visible on her face.

Once on her lunch break, she unfolded the piece of paper, and on it was written, "Please let me help you. Meet me at 5 p.m. and bring nothing but Steven with you. You cannot rouse suspicion in him, so you have to come as you are. My wife and I will help you and the boy to a safe place, and they will have all you need there." The address was way over the other side of London, but Katie knew that if she didn't go now, she never would.

As her shift finished at three, she had two hours to collect Steven and head off to what she hoped would give them a better and safer life.

"Come on, Steven," his Mum shouted. "We have somewhere to be." As he headed down the stairs for the last time, little did he know that he would never see the inside of that grotty flat again. The mould on the walls that his Mum washed weekly to try and stop his continuous cough, the tap in the bathroom that dripped endlessly all night long, and the people upstairs, like fairy elephants, all hours of the night. As Katie shut the door behind them, she prayed to God to keep them safe and for him to never find them.

As he walked into the refuge, the memories came flooding back. The fear, the excitement and the knowledge that good things happened here and that he was going to be a part of helping so many women overwhelmed him. He became a lawyer because he wanted to help people, and what better way to use his education and skills that he would never have had without the help of such people as the team he was about to meet for the very first time.

Chapter 46

Jessica readied herself for what she knew was going to be one of the hardest marriages that she was ever going to have to help come to an end. Isabella and Robert Collier were, for all intents and purposes, a tight-knit family. Only now had it emerged that Bobby, as his friends called him, had been cheating on his wife and family for decades.

Was there any truth in what she had been reading in the tabloids? Did Robert Collier have another family that Isabella knew nothing about? This was going to be a big case for Jessica and would, for the first time in her career, bring her name out to the forefront of the gossip columns and every magazine worth reading.

As Isabella stepped into her friend's chambers, Jessica could see the worry lines etched into her beautiful face. This was taking its toll on her, and Jessica had to make this as painless as possible. Yet, she feared there were more skeletons in Robert's closets than there were in the local graveyard. How was she going to cope once it all started to unfold?

"I knew I had seen that girl somewhere," Isabella said as she settled down in the big leather armchair opposite Jessica's desk. A warm coffee in her hands and the memory of Chloe Mallery clear in her head. It was a magazine article where this woman had come forward and said that she had a twenty-one-year-old daughter, and Robert Collier was her father. It was an old picture and a little bit blurry, but now thinking about it, she knew it was Chloe. She was one of Suzie's models, for Christ's sake she was so near and yet so far removed from them all.

The file Jessica had compiled had this article as pride of place, and she had shared it with Isabella so that she knew what to expect as the whole scenario unfolded. She had tracked Chloe down, and today was the day that the two ladies were to meet. Isabella had requested it; she needed to know if this girl was real. Did she really not have a clue about her stepfamily and their lives? With a feeling of utter dread, Isabella braced herself as there was a gentle tap on the door, and in walked Chloe Mallery. Her husband's eyes staring straight into Isabella's.

Isabella had a sudden urge to hug this beautiful girl; she saw immediately in her eyes that she had no clue who Isabella was, and she felt nothing but sorrow. Getting to her feet, she shocked not only Chloe but Jessica too, stretching out her arms to embrace the girl tightly. Letting her go, Isabella could see the tears flood into Chloe's eyes, and as they tipped over the edges of her eyelashes, it was like a floodgate opening. She sobbed and sobbed into her handkerchief until there were no tears left. All the while, Isabella had sat alongside her, rubbing her back, telling her that everything was going to be okay.

As she reached into her handbag, a pretty little Chanel creation that had been given to her at her last photo shoot, her mind racing and deciding yes, this was the right thing to do. The smooth, creamy envelope that she had held onto for weeks, taking the letter in and out, reading it over and over again, digesting every word. She knew that Isabella had to see this for both their sakes.

The air between them was still; you could hear a pin drop as Isabella read and re-read the words she knew were written by Robert. His sloping handwriting unique to him and him alone. If only he had told her, if only things were different. All Isabella could think of now were her children and how this news of a stepsister was going to affect them. She knew one thing for sure: they were going to know each other no matter what. Robert had kept his dirty little secret but no more, it was time to face the music.

Folding the letter back into the creases that were already well worn, Isabella placed it firmly into the envelope and handed it back to Chloe.

Without a word, she picked up her bag, gathered her thoughts, and said, "Come on, ladies, we are going out." As they left the chambers, a new feeling had swept over Isabella; she had a plan, and if it worked, the tabloids would leave them alone for good. All she had to do now was convince her children and Chloe that being a family was all that mattered.

"Taxi," she hailed as she flagged down the first black London taxi that came along. "Telford Parade Mansions, please, and hurry if you can." Jessica, astounded, just kept silent. She knew there was no point in trying to talk Isabella out of what she could only guess was going to be a face-to-face with all her children. This school half term was going to be one that none of them forgot in a hurry.

Chapter 47

Suzie had been rushed off her feet; the fashion show to beat all shows was scheduled for the twenty-fourth of the month, and it was fast approaching, with still so much to be done. Her assistant, Kelly, had been by her side for days, ticking off endless lists, checking and double-checking that everything Mary and Jordan Cleeve had requested was, in fact, being fulfilled. After all, this was as much their show as Suzie's.

Luther and his team had been fabulous, getting all the samples ready with time to spare. They were set, that very day, to sit down as a group and make the final cut for the show. If it all went to plan, their brand was going to blow the minds of the critics and cause a stir worldwide among the fashionistas. Suzie's designs matched with Mary's flair for colour and Luther's cutting skills; their pieces were exquisite and so on-trend that even the "couture whores," as Mary called them, would be flocking to buy off the peg.

They had chosen Rosenberg's as their meeting place for the day. Suzie's office just wasn't big enough, and her studios were far too busy to take one over for the morning. Mary and Jordan were making a long weekend of it and travelling down from Cambridge for a spot of lunch in the city and to catch a show at the Adelphi Theatre. Mary had been invited to a preview of the new musical, Kinky Boots. She had fallen in love with Charlie Price and his beautiful drag queen friend Lola back in 2005 when the movie hit the big screens. So, when the invitation arrived, she was thrilled to accept.

Their suite at the Lanesborough on Hyde Park Corner was exquisite. Jordan felt right at home in the splendour of it all. Dressed in their fluffy white gowns and matching slippers, they padded around, rubbing along nicely. The papers read, and endless cups of coffee consumed, and it was only seven a.m. They never slept in; Mary was up every morning at five, no matter what, and they loved nothing more than just musing over the Times crossword together. Mary would make up words, which made Jordan cross, but she would laugh so loudly that he had no choice but to join in. He adored his wife and could not imagine a life without her.

"We better get ready, my darling," Mary said as she planted a kiss on the top of her husband's head. As he looked up, he couldn't help but smile; he loved this woman with all his heart. Theirs was a love affair to remember and cherish. He was thankful every day for this beautiful creature that had stood by his side all of these years. They could teach the youngsters a thing or two about sticking to it and not giving up at the first sign of trouble.

"You look fabulous," they both said at the same time, chuckling to each other like schoolchildren. "We do indeed," he chimed, as Jordan twirled his wife around for a better look. Her outfit was sublime, a new design by one of their young new hopefuls, Connor Brady. He was fast becoming the best hire they had ever made.

"It's not too much for a breakfast meeting, is it?" Jordan held his wife at arm's length and made out as if he were critiquing her.

"Well," he pondered for effect, "the cut is superb, and the colour reminds me of that field full of poppies we stumbled upon in France," remembering the trip they had taken to Limousin in their earlier days. "No, my darling, not too much for a breakfast meeting at all."

Giving him the once-over, Mary gave out a long, low whistle.

"You have outdone yourself, Jordy," her pet name for him when they were alone. His navy suit with a shot of a pinstripe running through it complemented his eyes, and with the splash of red at his neck and a handkerchief to match, he was dashing. Mary knew, without even looking, that his socks would finish his ensemble. She smiled so broadly that he just wanted to kiss her.

"What was that for?" she asked as he released his wife, brushing down her trouser suit to release any wrinkles he had made.

"Just because," he said winking at her. One final finishing touch to add just a dash more colour to her lips, and they were ready to leave.

The taxi hailed, they headed off to Rosenberg's for breakfast. Fuelled only on coffee, they were both ravenous and were looking forward to the delights that their newfound family had in store for them.

The big meeting room at Rosenberg's was laid out like a banquet. The vast table set as if for a dinner party, and the whole family were there. The children all safely at school or with the nanny service they used when the need arose. The ladies had been busy the night before and woke up early for the final preparations, of not only the food but also to ensure that the mannequins for the preview had everything that they needed. Rosenberg's liked to do it the old-fashioned way and used their usual models all different shapes and sizes, to ensure that their lines would look good on everyone. After all, in reality, nobody was as a size zero, were they?

The hugging seemed to go on forever. Mary thought, *this is such a lovely warm place to be*. She and Jordan had never been blessed with children, so to see such a large family and their extended family all working towards a common goal-their goal-was a sight to behold. It was as if they had known each other forever, one big happy family doing what they did best.

Breakfast was already in the centre of the table so that everyone could help themselves. The array of different foods literally took their breath away. Suzie couldn't believe her eyes; they had even remembered that her favourite food in the whole wide world was peanut butter and bananas. There, perched on the edge of what looked like a mountain of fruit, were the freshest bananas and a crystal bowl filled to the brim with crunchy peanut butter. Squealing with delight, she was like a child in a sweet shop.

The chatter around the table was endearing to both Anna and Joseph, for they had created this business from nothing more than hard work and determination. Joseph hadn't been at work as he couldn't do it every day. He wasn't as young as he used to be, and Anna could see the long days were taking their toll on him. He loved it though, and came home every day regaling tales of the workforce and all that was happening at Rosenberg's. Keeping Anna abreast on who was courting whom and all the workroom dramas. *It's like a soap opera*, she thought to herself, *maybe I will write it all down one day!* Rosenberg's was his life, and here they were, sitting opposite some of the most influential people in the fashion industry. Placing his hand on top of Anna's, they sat in almost silence, just drinking in the atmosphere, pausing every now and again to squeeze each — other's hand. After all, words were not needed.

Jordan stretched over to help himself to a smoked salmon and cream cheese bagel, scanning the table with delight. There was so much warmth and love in this one room; he wished he could bottle it and take it home with him. He felt giddy with the joy of them all. Mary, seated to his right, was happily chatting to Esther about her time in the cutting rooms. The croissants and Emmental the ladies shared long since gone; they were now steadily going through what seemed like a field of strawberries. Fresh from Kent, Anna had told them they are the best.

Luther and Ada, looking like newlyweds, hadn't sat and had breakfast alone in years. Their little family took precedence, and they had forgotten how lovely it was to be just the two of them. Not Mum and Dad, just Lute and Ada, a young couple in love. Forgetting where they were, they chatted together, huddled like teenagers, hanging on each other's every word. Every now and then, they would stop to take bites of their double chocolate muffins, not really breakfast food. But this wasn't any ordinary breakfast, was it? Today was the day to step out of the norm and just enjoy the rewards of their labour. As they shared these glorious few hours, they both silently vowed to make more time for each other. This was what life was all about.

Isaac had never seen Lizzie looking so glorious, he thought to himself as he took a generous helping of cheese and fruit from the over laden platter laid before him. Ada had helped her to pick out a dress, and she had been to the hairdresser the day before. Her cheeks were glowing. Not one for makeup, she didn't need it; her natural beauty shone from within her. Choosing a plate of fruit as her breakfast, she really didn't enjoy food in the morning but didn't want to seem rude. It was nice,

209

she thought, to be out for a change and just be able to be herself. She missed her job in the bookstore but wouldn't trade her boys for anything in the world.

Immanuel had eaten his body weight in devilled eggs and freshly baked bread, and having excused himself to his hosts while he checked that everything was in place for the preview of the show pieces. He and Esther spent their lives together and alone, so they didn't need this time to reconnect. They did so love the family time, though, for they were godparents to Luther and Ada's children and took their responsibilities very seriously.

Eleven o'clock on the dot, and the big dividing doors were pulled aside into their hiding places, and to all their surprise, the preview pieces were ready to go. Immanuel taking his place back beside his wife, with a nod of his head, summoned for the show to begin.

The mannequins, one by one, boy, girl, boy, girl, like a line of school children on a trip, paraded the show pieces for all to see. There were gasps from Mary and Jordan alike, and Suzie was thrilled that they loved her designs so very much. This was a step into the unknown for Suzie, as designing menswear was a minefield, but here she was pulling it off with ease.

The claps and cheers as the last show stopper was unveiled could be heard downstairs in the cutting rooms. There stood before them was the most handsome and elegant couple they had ever seen. Standing bold and bright in their outfits that could adorn any situation, from a trip to the office or even an impromptu lunch. Suzie had nailed it; this was the pièce de résistance. Off the peg never looked better!

Recipe Six — Double chocolate chip muffins (Rebel Baker)

280g Plain Flour
75g unsweetened cocoa powder
2 ½ tsp Baking powder
½ tsp Bicarbonate of soda
½ tsp salt
250g Granulated Sugar
2 large eggs
300ml yoghurt
55g unsalted butter (melted & cooled)
60ml Vegetable oil
2 tsp instant coffee powder
1 tsp vanilla extract
170g choc chips & choc chunks milk & plain

Method:
Pre-heat the fan oven to 200 ºC, then line a muffin tray with 12 muffin papers.
Melt the butter in the microwave or over a bain-marie and set aside to cool while preparing the other ingredients.

In a large bowl, sift together the flour, cocoa, baking powder, bicarbonate of soda and salt. Add the sugar and mix together; set aside for later.

In a medium bowl, whisk the eggs & yoghurt, oil, melted butter, coffee and vanilla extract. Pour the wet ingredients into the dry ingredients and mix with a wooden spoon or spatula until just combined. Do not overmix; the batter should be thick and quite lumpy. Add the chocolate and stir.

Divide the batter into the 12 cases, almost filling them. Bake for 3 minutes and then reduce the oven temp to 180°C and continue baking for an additional 12 – 17 minutes.

Transfer to a rack to cool for 10 minutes before removing from muffin pan.

Chapter 48

"Mummy, you're home," Ava could have been heard down the street, her shrieks of excitement so loud, echoing around the apartment. As the lift door closed behind them, Isabella, Jessica and Chloe stood motionless for a moment. There, standing in the centre of the kitchen, was Robert. He looked a little dishevelled and was struggling for words as all three ladies entered the large expanse, Chloe standing to one side in fear of what he might do.

"Ava, darling, go along to your room for a little while, please," Isabella said without any emotion so as not to alarm her youngest daughter. "I will be along shortly, and we can have a proper chat then."

As Ava turned to go, she said, "Daddy, you will be here later, won't you?" With all the strength he could muster, he just nodded and smiled at his lovely Ava. All the while, Chloe had not taken her eyes off him.

"I wasn't expecting you to be here,", Isabella finally spoke to him, and he just shrugged, the words were lost in his head. Trying desperately to compose himself, he didn't understand. What was Chloe doing here?

Jessica was the first to break the ice. "Tea, I will make some tea," her voice trailing off long enough for Isabella to finally snap.

"Why didn't you ever tell me? All these years, and you kept this beautiful young lady from her family." Chloe could feel the anger oozing out of Isabella's every pore. "She had a right to know, we had a right to know." With that, running full pelt at him, Isabella punching, her fists flailing, she was now screaming at the top of her voice.

"You selfish, self-centred bastard," she yelled, at which point Chloe edged her way out of the room and in the direction that Ava had gone. Seeing the doors had name plaques on them, it wasn't long before she came face to face with her little sister.

Robert just stood there. He deserved all that Isabella was saying and doing, and he knew that the hurt ran very deep in his beloved wife, for he had been unfaithful to this kind, loyal woman their whole lives. Her anger dying, she composed herself and headed over to help Jessica, who had amazingly found her way around the kitchen and was placing the teacups onto a tray. She had even managed to find a packet of biscuits in the cupboard, a miracle in the Collier household with three children in situ. Jessica, giving her friend a knowing nod and a smile, directed them both into the sprawling open-plan living room and literally told them both to sit, as if they were in her chambers and had come for a meeting.

"Hello there," Chloe smiled as she spoke, felt the urge to hug Ava, but resisted the temptation and just stood in the doorway.

"Is Mummy okay?" Ava's question not easy to answer.

Chloe just nodded and said, "She will be!" Seeing that Ava was close to tears, she needed to tread gently. She didn't want to say anything that would jeopardise their future friendship. Asking what Ava was doing, she strode across the room and sat in the chair opposite the bed.

"Just writing in my journal. Mummy gave it to me on my last birthday, and I try to write something every day," she found herself saying to this perfect stranger. "Can I ask, please, who are you?" Before Chloe could answer, a door swung open opposite Ava's. Harry, after being in his room all morning, sauntered out into the apartment but was met with a frosty silence. Scurrying back to see Ava, he knew that she would know what on earth was going on.

"Oh, hello," he said to both of them but directed his gaze towards Chloe. "What's going on out there?" he said to Ava, wanting the answer to be simple and concise as he knew Ava could be.

"I don't know, but they have been shouting."

"Sorry, who are you?" Harry quipped, looking Chloe straight in the eye.

"A friend of your mum's, I just came to make sure Ava was okay once the shouting started; I know how frightening it can be to hear grown-ups argue," she said to both of them. This was turning out to be one of the strangest days that Chloe had ever had. Hearing the concertina lift doors open, all three of them looked up, and one by one, popped their heads out the door to see Amy and Lilly heading towards the kitchen.

Ava, taking the lead, headed out into the kitchen. She had a feeling that they all needed to be together today, and it didn't seem strange to her at all that Chloe was there with them. She just carried on chatting as if they had known each other for years.

As introductions were made, Amy, her sudden realisation where she had seen Chloe, said "I have seen you in a magazine. You were modelling a Crichton design that Mum ended up buying." Chloe just smiled and nodded. There would be time enough later on to fill them all in on who she actually was and what she did for a living. Chloe had no idea what they would say once they found out that she was actually their half-sister!

Jessica was first into the kitchen, her face a little ashen, and a worried look spread across it as she saw the expanse of the room. They were all here, and Robert was going to have to tell his story today. Isabella entered just before Robert, squished Ava's cheeks as she went past her, making her chuckle and squirm.

"Mummy, that really tickles," she laughed, and this broke the ice that was fast building as all the adults took their place around the large Island in the centre of the room.

"Wow, are we having a party?" Lilly asked with the biggest smile on her face that Chloe had ever seen. She was stunning and only thirteen years old, and look at her style, it was phenomenal. *Watch out world*, she thought to herself as she settled in for what she knew was going to be an emotional ride.

Robert, speaking for them all, just said, "No, it's great that you are all here together as I have something to tell you." All eyes were on him as he started to unfold his betrayal and deceit, telling them about Chloe's mum and how he had kept her a secret. He ventured into parts of his past behaviour since then and stopped with the latest story that had already hit the headlines. He had been fooling around with a woman half his age, and who Isabella thought, quite frankly, should know better; after all she was a politician's daughter and must have known the harm, she would inflict on herself and her Father.

"Wait a minute," said Amy, the eldest of his daughters. "So, you are telling us that Chloe Mallery is our half-sister?"

"Yes," came his reply, "always has been and always will be." The others were very still and very quiet, with Amy taking the lead with the questions.

"Mum, you had no idea?"

"No, my darling," Isabella lovingly said to her daughter. "This is all news to me too."

"And Chloe?" Amy implored.

"No, he only just told me about you all." Chloe felt tears pricking her eyes could feel the pain and hurt in

217

her new sister's voice. This was incredulous, how could they have a sister and not even know it?

"Dad, how could you?" Amy was beside herself with what felt like grief, but of course it wasn't. The anger poured from her now as she pushed her chair back and headed off into her new room, the first sight of the room that her mum and dad had created for her. Isabella rose to her feet, needing to see her precious daughter, the hurt she knew would be tenfold.

Jessica and Chloe busied themselves chatting to the other children, and Robert headed into the master bedroom to collect his belongings. He knew for sure this was the last time he would be in the presence of all his children.

Chapter 49

"It felt so good," Laura beamed as she told Nick all that had happened at the script meeting. "You inspired me to stand up for myself but to also stop thinking that I am owed something because of what I allowed him to do to me. I am a damn good actress, and I still have my job, without David Summers in tow." Their phone conversations sometimes stretching into the wee small hours of the morning, providing a place for her to be herself, just her and Nick. No pretence, and nobody to impress. Their talks bringing out the best in her and the even better in him.

Nick had always been a great listener, even when they were younger. How sad that she had never seen what was right in front of her face for so many years. She vowed to make it up to him and was planning how to see more of him in the coming months. Their schedules were crippling for both of them, but the quality time they spent together she was going to make damn sure was special.

Planning a trip to the Cotswolds, one of her favourite places in the whole world, Laura knew that the Lords of the Manor was going to be all that and more for both her and Nick. The meticulous emails to make sure that the room was perfect, the food was perfect and that they would both have their privacy. Being household names, this last part was the most important. She didn't want autograph hunters disturbing their intimate dinners and trips out in the countryside. No stone was left unturned, and Laura knew that this was exactly what she wanted and where she wanted to be.

Little did she know that David Summers had other plans. He was all for revenge. After all, she had humiliated him in front of his colleagues and people, he thought were his friends. He was going to show her, that was for sure. As the Daily Mirror went to press that very night, the headline read:

"Lauryl Simmonds of Josie's Law caught in the act"

Under the article was a picture of Laura draped over a top ITV executive at a gala event after-party that David had insisted she attend. His hand was clearly making its way up her skirt. What would the TV critics and bosses make of this?

Heading out in the early morning mist, their journey a long one, Laura wanted to get a head start on the drive. Her only thoughts were of Nick, as she swung into his driveway to pick him up. He was standing in the doorway, his face was pale, and he looked as if he wanted to throw up.

"What's the matter?" she said as she jumped from the car, leaving the door wide open.

Nick, holding out the paper, handed it to her and with a shaky voice whispered, "they are out to get you, my love," feeling a little guilty himself for his previous thoughts to ruin her.

As she scanned the page for an insight, she knew instantly who had done this,

"David Summers," she chirped. "I knew he was low, but by God, who knew he would stoop this low to make a point?" Turning around, Laura could see the car coming towards her, a photographer on either side, their cameras snapping and moving like yapping dogs hanging out the back windows. Why had she not thought about him retaliating and his revenge before this point?

Slamming the car door shut, she clicked the lock and headed towards Nick, his arms outstretched.

"It's all going to be okay, darling. You will see."

Allowing him to envelop her with his big, strong arms, she smiled into his eyes and said, "what can they do? They need me," or at least she hoped they did.

"I remember that night," she said to Nick. "He had his hands everywhere, and I ended up kneeing him in the balls," she almost spat out the words. *How sad*, she thought to herself, *that nobody had taken a picture of that.* Having told David Summers that night to tell his cronies to keep their hands to themselves, she felt deflated and as if all her planning had gone to waste. People could be so cruel. Or was this just karma coming back to bite her?

Nick knew that they would be hounded the moment they left the house, so he took charge and organised it all. They would stay there, and everything would be brought to them. Making a few phone calls, he managed to organise food, drinks and even entertainment in the shape of a large stack of DVDs that his sister was bringing round for them both. Telephoning their destination to announce their cancellation, forfeiting the deposit, Laura made her apologies but knew that this trip was never going to happen now.

"Let's face it all tomorrow," Nick smiled at her, leading her into the bedroom. She kicked off her shoes and settled in for the rest of the day. This time was for them, and nobody was going to ruin that.

Chapter 50

The twenty-fourth had come around so fast, Suzie literally didn't know what had hit her. There had been so much to do and so little time in which to do it. But here they were, the morning of the fashion show, and Suzie had roped everyone she knew in to help.

Greg was no exception, and he had been a godsend up to this point in the process. Having finished his last two chapters, he found himself at a loose end. Until he heard back from his editor with any changes needed, he was footloose and fancy-free.

"Do with me as you wish," he said, winking at her.

"You're on," she said, laughing and giggling all the while. She did love how this man made her feel. So, he and Ethel, jammed to the rafters with fabric, props and paraphernalia for the show, had made many trips backwards and forwards.

The venue, a quaint but roomy old hotel perched on the edge of the New Forest, which Greg and Suzie had found on their trip.

"It's perfect," she had told him as they sipped hot chocolate in the grand orangery, which Suzie had pointed out would make a splendid backdrop to their first show of the collection. Having said as much to the owners as they left, Suzie had finalised it all on her return. After all, they were there to camp, not work.

Kelly had been staying in the hotel for nearly a week, organising everything from lighting, sound, caterers, champagne deliveries and a whole host of other things. Her fiancé Grady had stepped in at the last minute to help too; his work having been a little sparse for the last few weeks. He literally just did whatever was on Kelly's list for that day and got stuck in. Suzie had managed to gain a sponsor in Laurent-Perrier and was looking forward to a glass of the sparkling pink bubbly once the evening got off to a start. *Who knew there was this much to do just to show off twenty-four outfits?* Kelly thought to herself as she ticked off a few more items from her endless lists.

The evening was being dedicated to all shades of pink, as the champagne was pink. Not the girly pink of babies and bubble-gum, but gentle pinks of all varieties had been chosen in the table linens, the drapes and the chair covers. No detail had been ignored, and every item had been designed to complement the next. Crystal of all shapes and sizes adorned the meticulously laid tables, and the silverware shone like mirrors from their set places. Handwritten place cards finished off with a gift for every lady in the room, and the night was set to begin.

Esther and Immanuel were on hand to ensure the safe delivery of the garments and for any final nips and tucks that might be needed as the show progressed.

"Everything is in place and ready to go," Kelly told Suzie as they sipped their coffees and put their feet up for ten minutes.

"From here on in, it will be what it will be," Suzie smiled a contented smile, knowing full well that her team had everything in hand, and they would not let her down.

The hotel was fit to bursting with the crème de la crème of the fashion world; Suzie and Greg holed up in the bridal suite as that was all they could get. The photographers already amassed outside, awaiting the entrance of, to name a few, Mary and Jordan Cleeve, the Rosenberg boys and Chloe Mallery, who was on the list as a mannequin way before the Collier saga. It was set to be an extravaganza like no other seen to date. Pitched as a forward-thinking collection for the average person on the street, today would pay tribute to the hard work and determination of so many people.

As they emerged from their rooms, the splendour they beheld was, Suzie thought, like watching a butterfly emerge from its chrysalis, unfolding itself to show its full beauty. The sleek black tuxedos and shiny black shoes complimented by the glorious colours of the dresses and accessories. Greg had taken some advice from Jordan and made his tie and socks fit beautifully alongside Suzie's outfit. Tonight, she was wearing a

225

Mary Cleeve creation, on loan for the evening as it was part of her own collection. The cerise pink ensemble with a fitted corset that nipped in at the waist and accentuated Suzie's ample bosom, leading to a full skirt. Its train a delicate scallop just tipping the floor as Suzie walked. Her shoes, a testament to time, had belonged to her grandmother, and were so delicate the silver bugle beads adorning the grey silk fabric catching every drop of light that landed on them. Kelly had made her a small clutch to match them, and she was so impressed with her skilled workmanship she was going to offer her a chance of designing her own range. Not tonight though, as there was enough to talk about but soon, without a shadow of a doubt.

Greg had chosen a striking cerise tie and topped it off with silver grey socks with a dash of paisley running through them in cerise. Jordan had told him exactly where to look; his dear friend Samuel Turner had been designing for decades, the mixes of colour and texture setting him apart from many of the other designers. The choices were endless. Suzie was thrilled with the final ensemble, and as she squeezed his hand, he wished her good luck and planted a little kiss on the end of her nose.

Shuddering all over at his touch, she just smiled, winked and said, "Later my love, we have the bridal suite after all!"

All eyes on the designer and her new man; the photographers swarmed around them, capturing their outfits from every angle. Suzie knew that they would be the talk of the glossies this week. Thank God for Mary and her collection; otherwise Suzie wouldn't have had a clue what to wear. Greg, ever the gentleman, led his lady out into the night, across the red carpet, and up into the orangery; his presence a calming influence on Suzie's tummy, which by now was in knots. She wished she could just do her job and not have to be centre stage. After all, she always used to say, "I would rather sweep the stage than be on it."

Most of the hotel guests were chatting and drinking the endless flow of Laurent-Perrier when Mary and Jordan Cleeve arrived, followed closely by the Rosenberg boys. Looking like a scene from an old black and white movie, Luther, Ada, Isaac and Lizzie, four abreast, headed up the red carpet. The ladies wearing Crichton designs from the couture collection had chosen well; Lizzie in a velvet midnight blue A-line gown and Ada shimmering from head to foot in a purple taffeta creation that had to be seen to be believed. Their husbands proud as punch as they escorted their wives to the top table.

Mary and Jordan, not wanting to take anything away from Suzie, were decidedly understated, both in black but still exuding the ever-present kudos of being two of the top designers of their time.

As the Master of Ceremonies called them all in to dinner, the doors closed to the orangery, and the show was about to start. Not your usual fashion show but a glimpse of twenty-four outfits being worn skilfully by the mannequins weaving their way in and out of all the tables, giving everyone a chance to get up close and personal with every stitch.

Chloe was first out into the room, and Suzie, knowing what had unfolded in the press, raised her pink champagne in salute as she walked past the top table; after all, it wasn't every day you found out you had a whole family you didn't know about. The press had run with this story so very fast, and it was as if a whirlwind had engulfed them all. Poor Isabella, she made a mental note to make sure she was all right before their lunch with Anna and Joseph.

As the evening went on, the mannequins swapped and changed and worked the room. There were a few hiccups, but nothing Esther couldn't fix; Jamie Stone, one of the male models that Suzie had hired, was struggling to fit into his outfit, a take on an old classic for the office. Suzie was braving the old-style hacking jacket with its leather patches on the elbows; this time mixing it up with some lighter fabrics that didn't automatically scream country gent. He must have been working out since his first fitting, but with a little easing of the stitching just for the night, Esther made it look fabulous. Teaming it with beautifully cut medium drill stone trousers, no socks and some suede loafers that matched the colour on the elbows, he looked set to go!

Some beautiful dresses for all occasions, the trouser suits designed and cut for a woman flowed beautifully as the mannequins moved, a sexy twist on a classic man's design. What woman wouldn't want one?

As the final pair came out, all other mannequins gone; these were the stars of the show. Chloe Mallery and Jamie Stone, hand in hand as they entered the stage. An evening wear twist for all to enjoy, and a show in the making as they danced together, the small wooden floor just up from the top table. Her gown, an exquisite cobalt blue raw silk, its drags and pulls in the fabric a testament to how it was produced. The fitted bodice hugging every part of Chloe's delicate frame, while the short full skirt skimmed her knees, showing off her beautiful long legs. Jamie, his twist on the formal suit in a beautiful two piece elaborately weaved charcoal check. The flecks of cobalt throughout matching perfectly with his eyes. Teamed with an open-neck cutaway collar shirt in pure white, he looked astonishing. Together, they were a sight to see.

As the dance came to a close, Jamie twirled his companion towards him, the music ending, he kissed her very gently on the mouth. Chloe was taken by surprise, as that hadn't been rehearsed, but she enjoyed the warmness he brought to her, even for a fleeting moment.

"Sorry about that." He smiled as he spoke. Back in the makeshift dressing room just at the back of the main dining room, Chloe struggled to remove her dress, and Jamie could see she needed assistance. As he eased the zip down the full length of her back, he couldn't resist

229

the urge to kiss her shoulders as the dress fell to her hips, revealing her beautiful skin. His kisses felt like warm rain drops on her skin, the sensations surging through her. Turning to face him, his eyes sparking, their blueness smouldering. She knew that she had to have this gorgeous man, but not here and not now!

"Thank you," she said, mustering all her strength to take a step back and busy herself with the task at hand. After all, they were professionals and being paid to do a job. Jamie, seeing her retreat, respected her silent wishes and steadied his nerve, leaving Chloe to her thoughts. Meanwhile, making a mental note to track her down for a drink when all the madness was over. Heading out into the orangery, a special table had been laid for those that had been requested to stay, allowing them to chill a little before meeting their hosts. To Chloe's surprise, it was just her and Jamie!

Chapter 51

"Sorry it's taken so long to arrange lunch," Isabella, knowing that Anna and Joseph were just happy they were all there, smiled and led the way to the kitchen. Jessica and Suzie trailed behind, looking at all the photographs that lined their walls. Years and years of memories, *pictures tell a thousand stories*, Suzie thought to herself. As she pondered one particular very old black and white photo, its edges well-worn and colour fading, she could see Anna approaching, all the while smiling.

Gently, she took Suzie's hand in hers and said, "That's my only picture of my parents back in Poland when I was a little girl; such a long time ago." Her memories taking her back to those days, her eyes filling with tears. Suzie hugged Anna close and could feel the strength this woman possessed. As she walked her friend out into the bright kitchen, she thought to herself, *this really is the heart of their home.*

The others already seated, a drink in hand. Suzie felt pleased to see all her new friends around one table.

Raising her now-filled glass, she said, "To friends, old and new." The cheers went up, and Joseph, ever the host, began to fuss over this table full of women, his smile stretching from one ear to the other.

They were in for a treat; Joseph was trying out some new recipes as he had been given a cookbook by Ada last Christmas.

"Five-hour lamb," he announced as he laid the enormous enamel casserole pot on the trivet Anna had laid down for him. "Jamie Oliver says you cannot fail," Joseph chuckled as he said it, praying inwardly that it all looked as it should. As he lifted the lid, the aroma was overpowering and made all their tummies rumble.

"Wow," Jessica said, "that smells divine. Is that red wine I can smell too?" Joseph set about spooning the contents into their oversized soup plates. He had kept them warm so that the food was piping hot as they got it.

"Yes," Joseph quipped, "Red wine, vegetables and everything all thrown in one pot and cooked for five hours. That man is a genius."

Anna had made some freshly baked bread, and as they all tucked into their food, the table came alive with chatter and laughter. They told their hosts everything that had happened, including the Chloe Mallery tale. Anna was aghast but soon calmed and realised that getting angry didn't help anybody. She wanted to give that Mr Collier a good talking to, though. She said out loud, and everyone laughed.

Isabella felt so comfortable in these surroundings. She had only known her new friends for less than a year, and they had become more important to her than anything. She knew as the divorce unfolded, she would need this tight-knit community and all the support that it offered her. As she scanned the room, she couldn't help but smile.

Jessica was a great listener and only felt the need to talk if she thought that what she had to say would hold any weight in the conversation. Her family law background was a great grounding for her, and she had learnt so much from the rantings and ravings of others. When to speak and when to hold back, it was a skill honed over the past decade and served her well.

"So, Suzie, I hear from Ada and Lizzie that your fashion show was a huge hit," Joseph enquired as the last remains of the lamb was being dished out between them.

"Yes, it will be in the glossies this week, so I will drop you in a copy to see." Suzie had been thrilled with the outcome of that night, and she was still fielding phone calls from prospective clients wanting her to shed light on their design teams. The Chloe and Jamie pairing caused a stir in the modelling world; she was glad that they were on her books!

As Anna busied herself clearing the plates away and getting the desert ready that Joseph had prepared, the ladies huddled and chatted, laughing always and sharing a bond that their hosts were happy to see.

"I couldn't eat another thing," Anna pointed her observation directly at Joseph.

He smiled his unbelievable smile saved only for her and said, "Of course you can, just not yet! We can wait and have another couple of glasses of wine before we tackle the pudding." The ladies raised their glasses, setting off a resounding cheer, and with that, Anna filled their glasses to the brim. She so loved having company.

"Joseph, go get the boys, see if they are home." Doing as he was told, he headed out into the lobby, first to Steven's apartment, then Greg's. As he rounded them up, he knew that Robert wasn't invited, and from what Isabella had said, he had moved out. Heading back to number two, Joseph rounded up more glasses, poured the boys a drink and watched on in wonder as Jessica came alive in Steven's presence. Greg, perched on the edge of Suzie's chair, just couldn't take his eyes off his beautiful girlfriend. As she became more and more animated, he thought he would burst with pride. Such precious gifts, friends are.

"So, Joseph," Greg chuckled, "what's for dessert?"

As Joseph cleared his throat to speak, Anna walked into the sitting room, saying, "Gluten-free apple crumble cakes anyone?" Balancing a huge jug of steaming hot custard in one hand and a plate piled high in the other, Jessica couldn't help but smile as she rushed to help Anna, thanking her for remembering. The cheers from the boys could be heard above everything else, as they all tucked in.

Recipe Eight — Gluten-free apple crumble cakes (Rebel Baker)

Crumble Topping:
180g Soft Brown Sugar
150g Butter
1tsp cinnamon
105g Plain gluten free Flour (Bobs Red Mill)
105g Gluten free Porridge Oats

Method:
Mix all the dry ingredients in a bowl and add butter. Rub with fingers to blend everything together; small & large chunks will appear, set aside.

Cake:
2 cooking apples (peeled and chopped into bite size chunks)
2 eating apples (peeled and chopped into bite size chunks)
1 tablespoon of lemon juice (to stop apples browning)
2 tablespoon of gluten free flour (to mix into apples)
230g butter (melted)
360g Golden Caster Sugar
1teaspoon of Vanilla
4 large eggs
350g gluten free Plain Flour (Bobs Red Mill)

4 teaspoons of gluten free Baking Powder

¼ teaspoon of salt

2 teaspoons of Demerara Sugar

Method:

Heat a fan oven to 180ºC

Line either a square or round baking tin with lining paper. A tall tin is required, or the cake will spill over.

Peel, core and chop apples; add lemon juice, coating apples to prevent browning. Mix in the flour; this stops the fruit sinking to the bottom.

In a large bowl, mix melted butter, sugar, vanilla and cinnamon. Mix in the eggs and whisk until blended and foamy. Fold in the flour, baking powder and salt. Gently fold in the apples.

Pour the mixture into the prepared tin, sprinkle the crumble mix on the top and then sprinkle the demerara sugar on top.

Bake for 45 – 55 minutes, cover with foil and bake for another 20 minutes.

Remove from the oven and allow to cool completely before cutting.

Delicious with cream, custard, or just on its own.

Chapter 52

"Everyone, this is Steven," the owner of the refuge said as they all huddled around the makeshift conference table. An old dining room table donated to them by a local resident, it served its purpose and somehow it belonged.

"Hello, everyone. I am sure I will eventually remember all your names, but for now, forgive me if I muddle you up." Sitting at one end of the table, Steven sat back to watch the meeting unfold.

There were ten families in total, and the overly large Victorian townhouse was home to them all. It was impossible to have more as there simply wasn't room. The idea was to help as fast as they could to find new homes and get each family settled to allow another to enter. This is where Steven would come in; his legal expertise would speed the process along and maybe even help them gain more sponsors from the local community.

As Steven sat and listened, he made notes and took down every detail he could about each family. He knew that he could just look all this up, but he loved the process of writing and listening. He remembered the lady that helped him and his mum; she had loads of notes by the time they were relocated and rehoused. He wanted to ensure that he could do everything possible to help and to aid every family that he could. From what was being said, he was going to have his work cut out for him. One family, in particular, his first, was a lady and her three children; all had been beaten and abused by their father, and Mum, by all accounts, had shielded them so often she had been to casualty over twenty times. Her bones might have healed and her scars faded, but the emotional and mental memories were another thing.

"First things first," Steven said, "Is mum ready to press charges against him?" The resounding yes brought a smile to his face.

"Thank God," he said. "She deserves to see him behind bars for what he has done." If only his Mum had been brave enough, he thought to himself, his dad would maybe have gotten help and not gone on to wreck other women's lives.

He had managed as an adult, unbeknown to his mum, to track down his dad, just to see if the pathetic man had changed. Much to his dismay, he came face to face with him in a pub one night in the East End. Of course, he didn't know his son. Why would he recognise the well-dressed, well-mannered man stood at the bar chatting to his companion? Steven had watched him for hours, bellowing at the top of his voice, drunk and pumping money into the slot machine that lit up the dingy bar every time he pushed the start button.

This memory spurred him on to find justice and make sure that some families, at least, could be shown a better life than the one they currently had. Directing his questions to one particular member of the team, he seemed to know so much about this family it made sense he would be the first port of call. Chester Collins was probably the largest man Steven had ever seen. He had to be six foot five, and he looked more like a hooker in the middle of a rugby scrum (his cauliflower ears giving him away somewhat) than a social worker. Softly spoken and with amazing diction, Steven found himself drawn to him, just to hear what he had to say.

Notes were written, and plans put into place. His first new case was about to unravel around him. Shaking Chester's hand, he assured him that the ball would be rolling as soon as he had spoken to the police. Then it was all down to the wife and mother to give her statement, telling Chester to get onto the GP and the local hospital for all her medical records. Steven headed up to the top floor to meet Nester Williams and her three boys for the first time.

Knocking quietly, Steven braced himself, as he had no idea what to expect or what exactly he was going to say. He was sure it would all come to him as the meeting progressed. Nester Williams opened the door and greeted Steven with the biggest smile she could muster. Her boys were ensconced on the sofa, all sat in a row, their best clothes on as if ready for church.

"This is Mr Sandgate," she said to them as she led Steven into the sitting room, hoping that he wasn't looking too closely at their lack of furniture and

239

possessions. She always patted down her creased dress as if she were wearing a delicate ball gown. Her soft South London lilt brought her voice to life and animated her face as she squeezed herself onto the end of the sofa, with a protecting arm going around her eldest boy.

Little did she know that Steven had an instant flashback to his first night at the refuge, where he and his mother, living in one room, had been placed for the time being, as the kind man and his wife had said. He could even remember how it smelled, and this shocked him to his core.

As if on cue, the boys stood up one by one and introduced themselves. Joshua, Steven found out, was five years old and liked trucks. Samuel was seven, and he was sad because he had to leave his friends and his school behind. Then there was Chad; he was nine but way older in his mannerisms, and he informed Steven that he was now the man of the house and that he would take care of his mother and brothers. This made Steven smile, and he vowed in his head to make sure that this little family would never be hurt again.

Gently and with an ease between them that Steven found endearing, the family opened up to him. Not surprisingly, there was anger, but they mostly just stuck to the facts, and it soon became apparent that this to them had been their way of life. Of course, they were sad but not bitter, which Steven found hard to comprehend as his own bitterness had all but consumed him.

Chad spoke for them all when he said, "Mum has always told us that one day an angel will come and save us all." They all inwardly hoped that Steven was that angel.

Chapter 53

Jessica couldn't believe it; the day was here for her to have the first fitting of her wedding gown. Suzie had been working on the design for a few weeks now, and the pattern cutters and finishers at Crichton's had been working overtime to get the dress to this stage. She hadn't wanted anything too flashy or poufy as she had called it, and under no circumstances did, she want to look like a meringue. She and Suzie had laughed and laughed at this final request.

"Not a meringue in sight," Suzie chuckled as she unveiled, for the first time, the sky-blue dress that Jessica had all but drawn for her, a vision from when she was a small child, always telling her Mum that she wanted to get married in blue. Her sudden intake of breath let Suzie know that she loved it.

The finest sky-blue duchess satin, Suzie had commissioned the bolt of fabric to be dyed as she wanted the colour to be just perfect for Jessica; its crisp folds accentuating as the off-the-shoulder straps enhanced every contour of Jessica's upper body. The fitted bodice leading to a full skirt, a split off to one side stopping at the thigh to allow her shoes to peep out.

These were exquisite and had been hand-beaded and embroidered by one of Jessica's friends. The bodice fastening at the back with more than forty of the most delicately hand-covered buttons Jessica had ever seen.

She stood for what seemed an age, just staring at herself in the full-length mirror. The blue was perfect.

Twirling around to talk to Suzie, she said, "At least I won't need something blue," to which they both laughed, breaking the tension a little. Jessica was near to tears, and Suzie, taking her friend's hand, helped her off the large platform that she was standing on and hugged her close, which made the tears flow fast and furious.

"What on Earth is the matter?" Suzie cooed at her friend.

"Honestly, nothing. I have never felt so beautiful and overwhelmed." Jessica, wiping her tears, smiled so widely she literally made her face hurt. "I love it," she said and popped herself back onto the platform for another twirl before the fitters got to work on the hem.

As they worked their magic, Suzie popped open a bottle of Bollinger. After all, it wasn't every day she had a hand in designing a friend's wedding gown. She had a few bottles stashed away in the fridge in her office for such occasions, and what a better way to celebrate the day? Sealing the cork back into its cage for Jessica to keep, Suzie filled four champagne flutes, two for them and two for the fitters. After all, they were all one big family. As she raised her glass and made a toast to the upcoming nuptials, they all cheered, and Jessica shed a few more tears.

"That's the gown sorted," Suzie said. "Let's head out into the square and get some dinner. I don't know about you, but I am starving." Jessica, not needing to be asked twice, stowed everything away in the fitting room for the final visit and grabbed her bag. As they strode with purpose down the stairs and out into the warmth of the spring evening, she knew that everything was just going to be perfect.

Chapter 54

Nick Cole had spent the whole day emailing, trawling and collecting evidence, as he had called it. *They are not going to get away with this*, he thought to himself. The story needed to be set straight, and after being holed up in his house for the whole weekend, sneaking out the back to escape the photographers on the Sunday evening, Nick knew he had to do something.

The prize came in the form of a video late on the Monday evening. He had all but given up hope that someone had seen her retaliate against the advances of that awful man. As it dropped into his inbox, he held his breath as it opened. There, in front of him, was Laura being manhandled by a rather fat and sweaty man in a crumpled suit. As he attempted to raise his hand up her skirt, she fiercely pushed him away from her, and with the swiftest blow, she kneed him square in the balls. To Nick's utter surprise, there was more; David Summers was also in the video, and he was shouting at her, telling her to suck it up if she wanted to succeed in this business. Laura, quite rightly at the time, told him she wasn't prepared to do that, and he was so angry he told her to leave.

What a gift this was. Now, how to share this so that all the world could see, and David Summers would be shamed forever.

Fortunately, Nick had many connections in television, radio and journalism. He also knew how to use the internet to his advantage.

"This is going to be fun," he said to Laura that night on the telephone. "Rest assured, when David Summers wakes up tomorrow morning, he will be out of a job." Nick almost spat the words out. Laura was overwhelmed with what this man was doing for her. After all she had done to him in the past, how was she ever going to repay him?

Securing an interview with the breakfast show on which he did his keep-fit segment, he and Laura were going into this with their eyes wide open.

"Once the video hit YouTube, the rest, as they say, will be history," he almost sang the words to Laura as they cut their way through the early morning London traffic. Nick had organised it all. As the video broke on the morning show, his friend at his gym was set to upload it onto YouTube. The press had already been informed the night before, and it was all systems go.

Laura was feeling very nervous.

"What if we bump into him at the studio?" she said to Nick as they approached the entrance, showing their passes that allowed them straight in, no questions asked.

"Don't be silly, when was the last time he turned up to an early morning meeting?" Nick was right, and she didn't even need to reply.

The butterflies in her tummy were doing summersaults, and she felt sick to her stomach. This one move was either going to make her or break her. She knew the all-boys club would band together to save David Summers, after all, he had friends in high places, or so he had always told her. As the minutes ticked by, she could feel the sweat building up on the palms of her hands, and her mouth felt like a desert. Pouring herself some water as she sat in the green room waiting for Nick to finish his segment, she closed her eyes and began to count her blessings.

"Miss Simmonds, they are ready for you in studio four." A young boy of about twenty was standing over her. As she opened her eyes, his smile captivated her and made her smile even wider.

"Thank you, Oliver," she said with ease, having read his name from his security tag. He was overcome that she knew his name and took her hand, helping her up from the large sofa that she seemed to have disappeared into.

"Three, two, one," the sound man did his final check, and they were off. After many questions and affirmations on Laura's part, it was time for the video to be played. Their viewers, normally in the millions, were set to see exactly how glamorous it was to work in television.

As the story unfolded both on screen and off, within ten minutes, the video on YouTube had garnered over one million hits. The Guardian had run with the story, albeit on page two, and of course it was over sensationalised in the daily rags. They had all been notified the night before so that the story could be released the next day. Thank God Nick had such a great relationship with the press. *David Summers was not going to know what hit him today*, Nick thought to himself.

"Wake up, you silly man," his wife's anger piqued at the thought that her husband had humiliated her yet again in the press. "You have really done it this time," she said as she threw the newspaper at his head. Striding out of the room, Elizabeth Summers picked up her suitcase and walked out of what was their family home. She couldn't bear to be there a second longer.

Nick and Laura, the show complete, just wanted some peace. They knew that once they set foot outside, the press would be on them. Scurrying through the myriad of tunnels that swept under the studios for large props and equipment to be moved in and out, they headed for the exit and out into the bright sunshine. A reprieve for now, getting into a waiting taxi, they sped across town to the legal offices of Porter and Dunne. After all, if Steven worked there, they must be good, Laura thought to herself.

Chapter 55

Rosenberg's had never seen such a turnaround in their order books. The fashion show had been a huge success for the boys, and their orders fulfilled to the distributers gave them time to concentrate on new clients and new designs. Joseph also had the task of making Steven's wedding suit still hanging over his head. The day was fast approaching, and they hadn't even sat down and discussed preliminaries.

Suzie had awakened in them a need to change, and they were embracing the changes with both hands. Joseph was enthralled to hear how well it was all going, and between them, Issy, Lute and Immy were soon becoming the new names on everyone's lips across the fashion industry. Being pegged as the new faces of fashion, they had joined forces with Mary, Jordan and Suzie, making their inner circle so tight that everyone wanted to join the party.

Taking on two new designers as part of their forward planning, Luther chose one himself, having seen her sketches over a coffee a few months previous. He knew that she was the right fit for their vision.

Amelia Barrett looking sharp, to say the least. Her shoes were impeccable, and her eye for design in an outfit was bar none. She exuded style and sophistication, and he remembered her as she had gone to the same university as him. After seeing her designs in her final showcase, he had hoped that one day she would do great things. Little did he know then that those great things would be expected by Rosenberg's.

The second a charming male friend of Isabella's. Simon Faith was a man's man. A sharp dresser, smooth talker and he loved not only his designing but was an avid cook to boot. He always said that there were only a few chefs in the world, the rest of us are just cooks! Isabella had joked that he was a catch for any lady when she recommended him. They had met up for lunch a while ago, Isabella apologising profusely for her absence in his life. They had once been close friends, and she had confided much in him about Robert and his misgivings. Never taking sides just listening and advising where needed, Simon was always there for her.

She knew he would be just what the men's department at Rosenberg's needed. His eye for detail, mixed with the invaluable lessons that Jordan Cleeve had taught him whilst on an internship during his university years, would set him in good stead with the boys on the team.

Joseph, having been tasked with the design and making of Steven's wedding suit, decided to involve Simon in the process.

"There is no point in making one man a suit at his own wedding," Joseph had chimed in one day at a design meeting. "Surely they all need new suits, not the same but designed in the same way." Joseph knew this was going to be an expense for the business to bear, but it was his business, so it didn't matter.

Simon jumped at the challenge, his first at Rosenberg's, and a chance to impress old Mr Rosenberg himself.

"Fabulous idea," Simon chimed as the buzz around the table became unbearable for Joseph to get a word in edgeways.

As he rose to his feet, he said, "Well, my boy, the ball is securely in your court, do your damnedest." Leaving them all to it, he strode out of the meeting and headed for the cutting rooms. Joseph was a tailor by trade and loved nothing more than just watching it all happen around him. He would walk around giving advice, helping if needed and nurturing his talented staff.

As Steven pulled up outside the Rosenberg's Studios, Joseph was just about to leave.

"Hello, my boy," he greeted him as he always had with this loving gesture. "I am leaving you in the capable hands of a new designer, Simon Faith. He is going to talk over your requirements, and we have a proposition for you too; I, of course, will handle all the tailoring for your suit as promised." With that, he waved his friend goodbye and set off up the road and back home to his beloved Anna, leaving Steven in the street a little curious.

"Hello there, you must be Simon," he stretched out his hand and greeted him with a firm handshake and a broad smile. Simon, smiling back, did all the necessary introductions and got right down to business, no messing about, just straight in.

"We have all been talking," he said, "and we agree that yes, you need a suit, but so do the other key men in your wedding!" Steven hadn't even given anyone else a second thought. He didn't even have a best man yet.

"Blimey," he said out loud, "I had better get my finger out if I want someone up there with me."

Simon just laughed and nodded, "Yes indeed, especially if we need to make them suits too." Laughing, they got on with the task in hand, choosing bolts of fabric, linings, handkerchief designs, shoes and shirts. Simon had told him to be able to design a suit, you need to know what else is involved to tie them all together.

Measurements taken and everything chosen as far as fabric was concerned, Steven assured Simon that he would have a best man by the end of the week. Surely it couldn't be that hard to persuade someone to do it for him? He had the perfect candidate in mind; he just had to ask the question and hope that they would say yes.

"Did you get it all sorted?" Joseph said as Steven headed across the lobby, making him jump a little as he hadn't noticed him coming out of the front door with the little watering can that Anna usually used for her well-tended window boxes.

"Yes, thanks Joseph, Simon was really helpful, and it really was quite easy to choose once we had decided on accessories etc."

"That's good, my boy," Joseph chuckled as he went back inside his apartment. He could hear Anna calling him as his coffee was ready. Smiling, Steven headed up the steps two at a time. He wanted to shower and change into something comfortable; he had a lot of thinking to do.

Chapter 56

Suzie, letting herself into Greg's apartment, exclaimed at the top of her voice, "What is that heavenly smell?" Heading straight into the kitchen, she could see Greg just about to retrieve a tray of scones from the oven. The music blasting from his iPod was deafening, so she turned it down a little. Without turning around, he told her to pop the kettle on, and he would be with her in a minute. Dropping her key into her pocket, she tapped it lightly for reassurance; Greg had given it to her a week ago, and this was the first time she had been brave enough to use it.

Seeing that the table was set for what looked like a formal high tea, Suzie's face turned a little red.

She turned to look at Greg, and with a flutter of hesitation, said, "Sorry if I am intruding on your plans. It hadn't entered my head that you might be busy." Her hands shaking a little as she filled the kettle at the oversized butler sink. Its copper structure, when filled with water, made it extra heavy.

"I do love this old kettle of yours," she said as she placed it on the already lit gas stove.

Putting the scones onto a large wire rack to cool, Greg strode across the room and took her into his arms. His kisses were divine, she thought to herself. He always seemed to know exactly what to do to make her feel loved, nibbling gently on her lips as he kissed her sensually, knowing just how to make her shudder with delight. Not wanting to release him just yet, she laid her head on his chest and drank in the scent of him.

"You smell like you," she said, her smile spread wide across her face. Looking up into his eyes, she could see he was happy too. Their ease and sense of comfort with each other building in strength each and every day.

"Don't be daft, I was literally just going to call you and invite you down for tea and scones," he said, pulling out her chair and acting as if he were her butler.

He draped the tea towel he was holding over his arm, and with a very British accent, said, "My lady, I am having friends over, and I am so glad that you are here too." He chuckled to himself as he opened a napkin for her and laid it gently in her lap. Kissing the top of her head for good measure, he headed for the front door to leave it ajar for his friends.

She could see that Greg had made scones, of course, and he then went on to tell her that they were gluten-free.

"So, your friends are Jessica and Steven, I suppose," she said smiling as if her detective skills were on par with Sherlock Holmes.

"Of course, they are," Greg laughed at the expression on Suzie's face. "Steven called last night and said that he had something very important to talk to me about." Suzie, having not eaten anything since the day before, scanned the table and could see that there were two different flavours of jam and the biggest pot of clotted cream that she had ever laid eyes on.

"I made that myself," Greg said with the biggest smile on his face. She really was in awe of his ability in the kitchen. Suzie, being more of a main course cook, her baking and dessert skills left a lot to be desired. "By the way," Greg said as he finished his preparation of the table, "they are our friend's, not just mine." This one statement made Suzie very happy.

They were so busy chatting neither of them heard their guests pad across the hallway. Having taken off their shoes at the door, Steven and Jessica followed their noses and knocked loudly on the frame to the big kitchen door, making both Greg and Suzie jump out of their skins. All four fell about laughing.

"We could have burgled your flat, and you wouldn't even have known," Steven said, the jollity in his voice making light of a serious situation.

"Yes, I know," Greg said. "I often leave the door open and then think I shouldn't have."

They had become really good friends, all four of them, as there were no pretences between them. Jessica relaxed completely in Suzie's company, and she really loved Greg's sense of humour.

As the ladies chatted happily, Steven braced himself and said, "Hey Greg, I don't suppose you would do me the honour of being my best man?" The look on Greg's face was a picture.

"Me, your best man?" he said, shocked and stunned. "Wow, I would be happy to. If you are sure?" The relief on Steven's face was there for all to see, as he had no family, only his mum, and he hadn't really forged any long-term friendships as a child as they had moved about quite a bit as he grew up. Greg really was his first best friend.

"Are we having these scones or not?" Suzie almost scolding Greg for making them all wait, her tummy rumbling in anticipation.

"Of course, of course," Greg said. "I was just making sure they were cool enough to eat first. I know how much you love my buns." Tapping his bottom as he said it made Suzie blush, and she giggled with embarrassment. Asking each in turn to hold up their plates, Greg placed an oversized scone on each one, telling them to slice them in three as they tasted better that way. He wondered to himself, *would it be jam first or cream?*

Recipe Nine — Gluten-free scones and clotted cream (Rebel Baker)

350g Gluten free flour (Bobs Red Mill)
1 teaspoon of gluten free baking powder

85g Stork or butter (hard and chopped into cubes)

2 – 3 tablespoons of sugar

85g raisins (optional)

150g plant milk

25ml plant cream

1 tsp pure vanilla essence

Squeeze of lemon juice

Plant milk to glaze

Method:

Preheat the oven to 220°C

Place the flour and baking powder into a large bowl and mix well. Add chopped Stork or butter and either mix by hand or with a bread hook to form breadcrumbs. Stir in the sugar.

Place plant milk and cream into a glass jug and heat in the microwave for 30 seconds. Add the vanilla and lemon juice and set aside.

Place two baking trays into the oven to heat.

Make a well in the dry ingredients and add the liquid from the jug.

Quickly combine the ingredients until they are just coming together and remove the rough dough onto a floured surface.

Sprinkle lightly with gluten-free flour and fold into itself two or three times until it looks smoother, but do not overwork the mixture. It should not look perfect.

Bring the dough into a round shape, approximately 4cm deep, and sprinkle with flour. Using a smooth-sided cutter, and making sure you do not twist it (this action will prevent it from rising if you twist), cut out your scones.

Reform the dough gently into a round shape and repeat.

Remember, do not overwork the dough.

Brush the scones with plant milk and place them on the heated trays quickly. Put them straight back into the oven and bake for 10 minutes until they turn golden and rise. They should sound hollow when tapped on the underside when they are done.

Top the scones with jam and cream — or is that cream and jam? You decide!

Chapter 57

Crichton's was ticking along nicely. *I really am lucky*, she thought to herself. Her team was so loyal and dependable. Kelly, her assistant, she had known for a while, deserved a little boost. After all, she had been with her right from the start, championing her on, never really asking for anything more than just being part of the team.

Her bag designs had flourished, and they really did need to be brought off the paper they had so lovingly been drawn on and into the cutting rooms. The very idea of a Kelly Moore bag being distributed through not only Crichton's but Rosenberg's and the Jordan & Cleeve brand was beyond a dream.

Grady Kilgallon, Kelly's fiancé, had helped pull it all together, and he couldn't believe what Suzie was about to do for them both, really. Being a scriptwriter and part-time actor, he knew that they struggled some months to makes ends meet. Kelly always told him that he had to follow his dreams and be the best version of himself that he could be, never once worrying that she didn't have all she needed or wanted.

Grady was always on hand whenever they needed help, setting up fashion shows or just fetching and carrying. He had put up with so much over the years with late nights and early mornings. Suzie knew that this was the time to pay it forward.

After calling a meeting of all staff for four p.m. Suzie knew that Kelly would be the first one there. After all, she was in charge of all that stuff, so she had to turn up, really. Making sure that her diary was clear for the day, she was free to just sit back and enjoy, what she hoped was going to be one of the best decisions she would ever make.

"What do you think it might be?" Delores from the cutting room could be heard saying over the top of everyone else. Virginia, Suzie's long-standing production manager, tried desperately to shush her. She really should have a word in private about how to behave at such meetings as this one. She didn't know herself why they were there, so was sure Suzie had kept whatever it was close to her chest to stop any gossiping among her workforce.

The cutting and finishing rooms at Crichton's were as busy as they had ever been. These new designs for Rosenberg's had brought about so many new customers and fashion shoots. Suzie and her team worked around the clock to ensure that everything a customer wanted, they got.

Virginia had been there from the get-go, some weeks never getting paid, and others in abundance.

Eighteen years her senior but the funniest, maddest and most patient friend she had ever met. Both on the same course at university, but taking completely different routes when they finally finished. 'Gina,' as Suzie most lovingly called her, was in for a surprise too. She couldn't help but smile at her friend across the room as she mothered all the young pattern cutters and fussed over how the room looked for the meeting. Suzie hadn't even told Grady that his Mum was getting a surprise too.

Suzie always liked to have her full staff meetings in amongst the workforce. She said it helped her to think, and she felt at home there with them. Crichton's was one big happy family, and she hoped they all knew how much she appreciated them. Maybe today would show them exactly what she truly felt. As the trays of champagne glasses were carried into the room there was a sudden buzz that went all around and then just as suddenly, they were in complete silence. Suzie tapping the side of her glass commanding their attention immediately.

The smile spread across Suzie's face as she looked on in awe at her most cherished friends and co-workers. Unfolding the beautiful, crisp white paper her lawyer had drafted for her that very week, she could feel the winds of change sweeping over her, and it brought her so much comfort. As she cleared her throat and took a very large swig of her champagne to steady her nerves, she began to read the letter that would bring about a whole new dimension to Crichton's. "To you all. Thank you for coming today to this very special moment in Crichton's history. As you all know, I started this company a few years ago now, and it has moved on further than even my wildest dreams. Forging an alliance with both Rosenberg's and the Jordan & Cleeve brand has made me realise that I really couldn't have done any of this without you all.

"With this in mind, I have decided to share my company with you all. My proposals are as follows: Virginia Kilgallon, you will now own fifteen percent of Crichton's. Kelly Moore, you will now own fifteen percent of Crichton's, and we will be finalising the development of a new and exciting Kelly Moore bag brand. To everyone else you will receive shares in Crichton's across the board to the value of ten percent collectively. I hope this small dividend will reap you all rewards."

"I will hold sixty percent of the shares in Crichton's and the final vote sits with me and me alone. I will be more than honoured to have my two best friends by my side, the three of us making decisions and carrying Crichton's forward into new and exciting times."

"Now, please raise your glasses, as I feel there may be a few tears and much joy!"

The cheer rang out across the cutting and finishing rooms, and the buzz of excitement was electrifying. Kelly literally had to steady herself in disbelief. Never in her wildest dreams did she think that today was going to end this way. Grady had been hiding in the wings, ready and waiting to celebrate with his fiancée, and Gina's husband, Paul, dressed in his best suit, had pulled out all the stops, bringing his wife a dozen orange roses and the biggest smile she had ever seen.

"Wow, I am lost for words." Kelly hugged Suzie so tight she thought the breath would be taken from her.

"You deserve it," her friend said with the biggest smile she could muster. Seeing Gina heading in their direction, they both opened their arms, and a group hug prevailed. The tears from all three of them now flowing freely, and Suzie couldn't help but feel elated. She had taken the reins for so long; it would be good to have some vital help, and what better than from her two best friends? As the room came alive, the champagne flowed, its bubbles paling into insignificance against the excitement they all felt.

It was Gina's turn to speak next, and she did so with such clarity and professionalism, tapping the side of her glass with her spectacles, which were dangling where she could always find them around her neck.

She said, "It has been my utmost pleasure to watch this company grow and to work alongside such great friends, I think when I speak I do so for us all when I say hip-hip hooray for she is a jolly good boss lady." As the cheers rang out across the whole of Crichton's, they all knew that this was the start of something amazing. Kelly just shook her head as if to say, 'No talking for me,' and raised her glass in salute to her friend, mouthing the words 'thank you' for Suzie alone to see.

Chapter 58

"Isabella, how are you holding up?" Suzie said with a hope in her heart that her friend could cope with what was coming out of the tabloids.

"You know what, at this point, nothing is surprising me," she said with a very heavy heart, not so much for herself, but for her children who were watching from the sidelines as their parent's marriage unfolded for all to see.

After Amy and Isabella had seen the front cover of that magazine on their fated shopping trip that day, Isabella kept racking her brains to remind herself where she had seen the young woman her husband, Robert, was kissing. The sudden realisation that it was, in fact, Holly, Max Brompton's mistress and now soon-to-be new wife was more than she could bear. Those ice-blue eyes looking lovingly into Robert's would forever be in her dreams.

"Suzie, what about the baby? Is it Max's or Robert's?" Isabella, finding the courage to say this out loud for the first time in months, was glad that it was finally out of her head.

"I wouldn't like to hazard a guess," Suzie said, shaking her head and wondering what Max was thinking about it all.

"Put it this way, I would love to be a fly on the wall for that conversation." Suzie laughed so hard she couldn't stop. Karma was a bitch and had serious debts to pay. "Sorry, darling, I didn't mean to laugh quite so hard, but this little web of deceit seems to be encompassing so much more than was once thought."

Isabella couldn't help but join in with her friend, laughing at first, but soon the tears flowed freely and for the first time in a long time, she grieved the loss of her marriage, her husband and the life she foolishly led alongside him. It was almost cathartic, and any number of hours spent in a counsellor's chair paled into insignificance as she let her feelings flow from her. *Who needs therapy when you have friends*, she thought to herself?

As Suzie strode across the room, she put out her arms and cradled her friend to her. She didn't remember how long they stood there, but she allowed Isabella to just sob.

As the sobs subsided, she held her at arms-length and said, "Come on, let's go get a drink. I think you deserve one!"

As they headed towards the lift, Suzie couldn't help but smile. Amidst all the chaos, Isabella looked faultless in a Crichton creation and carried herself with such grace and ease. Everything, she thought, was going to be okay; she could feel it in her bones.

As the concertina gate was pulled open, Suzie could see Anna sitting on her little wooden chair tending to her flower boxes.

"Hello, girls," she said with the biggest smile on her face. "I have my babies here today, and all the grandchildren will be here together later on. It's such a blessing, you know, being able to be part of their lives." As they chatted for a few minutes, Isabella thought about her own mother and how she would have loved the children. Thinking then about Winnie, having missed the last few months with the children, she wondered when they would all see her again. Grandparents were so very important, and their wisdom they imparted was invaluable.

"Don't spoil them too much Anna!" Isabella shouted as they headed across the lobby and out into the morning sunshine. Anna waving her farewell, knowing that without a shadow of a doubt, she would spoil them..

Chapter 59

Jessica was so busy; her wedding plans would have to wait for a few more weeks. Porter and Dunne was buzzing with so many new clients. Nick Cole from one of the leading breakfast shows had hired one of their top entertainment lawyers. His girlfriend was bringing forth a sexual harassment claim against one the executives from the network they both worked for. She had seen the videos airing across the internet and knew that this was going to bring the firm a lot of publicity in the near future.

For herself, it was the wife of this very high-powered executive that she was dealing with. In her opinion, she needed Isabella, as she specialised in such high-brow couples. Knowing that Isabella had so much on her own plate, she accepted the brief but was feeling a little out of her depth as she worked to keep harmony with her clients and not take one to the cleaners, as was Isabella's reputation.

Elizabeth Summers was a very petite and beautiful lady, mid-fifties, and to all intents and purposes, she epitomised a lady who lunched. Her dress sense was impeccable, and she carried herself with such dignity

Jessica found it very hard to understand why a man would cheat on her. Who knew what went on behind closed doors in any relationship? She was about to unfold their lives and lay them out bare to figure out how to help her client and cause as little turmoil as possible. After all, she thought to herself, it wasn't in her nature to fight dirty. Or was it?

"Elizabeth Summers for you, Jessica," her paralegal announced as she showed her into Jessica's chambers. She loved her room; it was quaint and inviting, every piece of furniture hand-picked and lovingly placed to show collectively that they made a statement.

"Great room," Elizabeth said as she chose one of the deep-buttoned Chesterfield chairs on the other side of the large sprawling desk. It creaked as she sat down, and she noticed the years of wear on the arms. So many people had sat there before her, she thought; were they as nervous as she was?

"Can I get you anything, Elizabeth?" Jessica began, and as she spoke, she could feel the tension dissipate a little.

With a huge smile, her client said, "Call me Beth; everyone does." There and then, Jessica knew she wanted to help her new client and would do everything she could to make it as painless as possible.

Formalities over and putting Beth completely at ease, she began to unfold the endless treacheries of deceit and cheating that she had ever heard across her career. That was a lot of divorce, *but this one knocked them all into a tin hat,* she thought to herself.

Stopping mid-sentence, she couldn't help but say, "Why have you allowed this man so publicly to diminish your worth?" It made no sense to Jessica, and she was always shocked to hear how many women just put up and shut up.

"Simple," Beth mused, "I have nowhere else to go." That statement alone made Jessica feel so very sorry for her. How many other women were living their lives alongside a man because they didn't feel brave enough to ask for more?

Jessica thought back to her own mother's advice to her, which was clear and succinct, and to the letter. "Some people are together just so they are not alone. Some people want magic. Be one of those, my girl, and never settle."

It turned out David Summers had been cheating on his wife for over twenty years, in and out of the spotlight. She had allowed him to continue to humiliate her because he had convinced her over time that she wasn't worthy of love. Yes, she had everything she wanted materially, but nothing as far as love and a family were concerned. Never being blessed with children, she had nothing really, just stuff and a few friends whom she really couldn't count on at all.

Jessica could feel the inner sorrow of this very lovely lady, buried deep. Her barriers so intact it was going to take a miracle to encourage her to release the fear and the self-loathing that she had built up over the years. Her determination would somehow, with grace, allow Beth to see that she was worth more and could forge a better life for herself. After all, wasn't that what life was all about?

David Summers' latest misdemeanour had caught the headlines in more ways than one. It wasn't so much that he was cheating, but he was encouraging men to harass, and in some ways, abuse their standing and take advantage of the young actresses in their care. This, in itself, was deplorable, and he had been seen many times with Lauryl Simmonds from his hit show, Josie's Law. So many lessons needed to be learned, not only by the men but also the actresses, about their worth and their self-respect.

As the story unfolded, Jessica took notes, taped snippets of the conversation and assured Beth as they went along that none of this was of her fault and she had nothing to be blamed for. Jessica would make sure this lady got everything that was owed to her and more. Additionally, she needed to help her to get some help and find a purpose in life. Jessica had just the idea in her head. That conversation could wait for another day, but if she could convince Beth, they could start something that would help so many women across all walks of life. She knew this could be just what was needed to give her some purpose.

As their meeting drew to a close, Beth could feel the tension easing from her body. She had finally told

271

someone about her plight, and they were going to help her. As the smile spread across her face, she knew in her heart that everything needed to change, and it all had to start with her.

Chapter 60

"Come on, Kenny!" Chester shouted as he headed down the stairs of their lovely little townhouse in Chiswick.

"Okay, okay!" he shouted back, "I am just finishing off this marking before we leave." It was all right for Chester, Kenny thought. He didn't have thirty-five degree students relying on him and a final show to prepare. Kenny Phillips was the Deputy Head of Drama at a leading performing arts school nearby. The pressure of the job was taking its toll, so Chester had suggested as they both were having hard times, that they should head out for the day and enjoy the sunshine, meeting friends later for food.

Covent Garden was their destination, and some rest and relaxation with new friends he had met at the refuge was just what the doctor ordered. Steven Sandgate and Jessica, his fiancée, was meeting them for lunch at a little bistro that Chester had been dying to try for ages. It specialised in gluten-free food, and as a coeliac, he was forever looking for just the right place to eat out.

It was a bit of a trek on the train and tube, but they were well-versed in the London life they so very much loved, and they both enjoyed making up stories about the train dwellers as they played the game "shag, marry, or avoid". It made them howl to themselves, the other passengers not having a clue what made these two very beautiful men laugh so hard. Chester Collins was a giant of a man, gentle, kind and exuded sex appeal. He was born in London to two very industrious parents, Ajay & Atia, who had travelled from India many years before. Neither knew what this new country would offer them, but they wanted to make a family and for their family to be safe. Having succeeded, they were now the proud owners of a portfolio of houses that stretched from one side of London to the other. Their tenants ranged from teachers to bankers, and they treated them all with respect and took care of their properties as if they themselves actually lived there.

Chester had worked in various different departments as he studied for his degree in health and social care at South Bank University. Seeing for himself how much work actually went into running a successful business, it gave him a work ethic like no other. His parents, their love ever present where their son was concerned, could not have been prouder of the man that he had become. His mum knew from an early age that her son was gay, but she allowed him the space and time to grow and decide for himself the right time to tell her and his dad.

Ajay, her husband, had at first taken the news as some kind of slight on himself. Had he failed his boy somehow? When Chester sat them both down, he explained it wasn't a choice. He hadn't woken up one day and thought it would be fun to be gay. It was in him; it was who he was. Their acceptance had been a relief to Chester, and he hugged them both so close he took their breath away. After all, he knew only too well from Kenny that not every man had this reaction to their life choices.

Kenny Phillips, his partner of seven years, was, he knew, his soulmate. They had met at school when they were just boys, twelve and thirteen to be exact, establishing a friendship that was still with them to this day. Back then, they were inseparable and loved nothing more than making dens, exploring the surrounding woodland and spending endless hours at the local park. Just friends enjoying the company they offered each other and nothing more.

As secondary school came to a close, they drifted a little as they attended different colleges. Always coming back together for nights down the pub and family gatherings. Their parents were great friends and loved nothing more than having grand parties and get-togethers. Their romance developed one night at a party at Kenny's parents' house. They had ended up in his room getting ready for the evening, and Chester found himself staring endlessly at this beautiful man standing before him. They were nineteen years old, and it hit them both like a train. Kenny, a drama student and ever the entertainer, was reciting the balcony scene from Romeo and Juliet.

As he said the words, "Romeo, Romeo, where for art thou," his eyes met Chester's, and he knew from that very moment that he loved his best friend with all his heart.

His hazel eyes penetrated into Chester's, imploring him to feel the same. His bare chest exposed as he placed his arms into the crisp white shirt he had chosen for the evening was more than Kenny could bear. As an Indian man, he was encouraged to wear what his parents called proper attire, so his Nehru jacket chosen for the evening would complement his new shirt beautifully, its colour bringing out the flecks of brown in his eyes.

Before he could place each of the mother-of-pearl buttons into their respective buttonholes, Kenny had crossed the room and taken him into his arms. Their kiss was soft and sure and for both of them, it was the first kiss they had ever had with anyone. Fumbling a little but soon finding their stride, the passion inside both seared to the surface with such abandon that they were both shocked at the sheer joy of their union.

A loud tap on the door pulled them back to their senses, and they moved to each side of the room faster that Chester had ever run with a rugby ball in his hand. As Chester's mum entered with a couple of glasses of champagne for them both, she smiled and inwardly thanked God for them finally realising they were made for each other,

"Hello, you two. I thought you could use a drink as its looking and feeling pretty stuffy down there," her wink to them both assured them that she knew and was fine with it. Taking her leave and closing the door firmly behind her, she could not have been happier for them both.

As the train pulled into Charing Cross, they both grabbed their coats, smiled at one another and walked steadily along the platform towards the exit. Covent Garden was just a stone's throw away, and they had ample time to meet their friends.

Steven and Greg had already arrived, and Jessica was heading that way too with Suzie in tow. They had been out in the morning to finalise the bridesmaid dresses, and it seemed churlish not to invite them both along. Chester and Kenny wouldn't mind. It was going to be a great day filled with people-watching, food and wine. What else did they need?

The restaurant was fairly quiet when they were finally all there together. Their ease with each other was a sight to see. Anyone looking in from the outside would never have known that they literally had only just met two of them and that their friendships were all quite new.

"One rule," Steven had said right at the start of the meal. "No talking shop, or religion," laughing as he said the last one, and they all nodded in unison as the wine was poured out across the table. Jessica, being the host, they all raised their glasses, and a resounding cheer rung out loud and clear.

Chester and Kenny, not needing the constant reassurance that the other was there, found their new friends' company both enlightening and entertaining, to say the least. Greg was on form, regaling tales from the party that saw an end to Max, rejoicing in his good fortune as the new man in Suzie's life. Jessica was all that and more with her stories of her university days and the student union antics that she would never forget as long as she lived, or so she said. Steven and Chester had a quiet understanding between them as Steven shared a little information about his childhood and how he got to where he is today.

Suzie and Kenny were getting on famously, and she promised to come and see his show. As they were discovered chatting about work, they had to pay a forfeit. Both standing at this point, they had to drink their whole drink with the other hand that wasn't usual to them. Luckily, Suzie was on a water round, but poor Kenny had a whole pint in front of him. Taking his time, he lifted the glass and slowly downed the contents to the end. Feeling very bloated and sick, he rushed to the loos and proceeded to throw the lot up. The cheers from their table got louder and louder, and the waiter very politely asked them to consider the other diners.

"Serves you right," Chester said, hugging Kenny to him.

Laughing, Kenny took his seat and said, "Right who wants to talk work?" As the courses came and went, the wine flowed, and the easiness just got better.

These six truly had bonded, and they were all planning various different get-togethers as the evening came to a close.

Chester, all but holding poor Kenny up, said their goodbyes, and turning to Steven said, "See you at work on Monday, we have a big week ahead of us." Numbers swapped and hugs all done, they all headed out into the night and in opposite directions.

"I think Charing Cross can do one", Chester said, hailing a taxi and bundling Kenny safely into the back seat.

The four jumped into another taxi and headed towards the Mansion House. They were all very tired and a little worse for wear.

"Anyone for a nightcap?" Greg said as he winked at Suzie.

"Honestly Greg, I feel exhausted and all I want to do is climb into bed and sleep," Jessica said, snuggling into Stevens side.

"Thank God you said that," Greg smiled "I haven't been out in such a long time I had forgotten how tiring it all was."

Chapter 61

Isabella and Simon had been friends for years, so going out for a drink and a meal was nothing out of the ordinary for them both. Arranging to meet at his house in the sleepy little town where he resided on his weekends off, he organised it all. A car would pick her up from the Mansion House and bring her to him, but he told her to pack a bag as she could stay at his for the night and go back the next day.

Having done this numerous times in his London flat over the years, she wasn't fazed at all. But when it came to packing, Isabella got into a state. Asking Suzie what she should wear and what she should pack.

"I feel like I am going on a date and am terrified all of a sudden," she confided in her friend. Taking the reins, Suzie chose outfits, accessories and underwear for Isabella as she felt her friend needed a little guidance in the right direction.

Her bags packed and waiting in the foyer, she felt a knot her stomach that was increasing in size; why was she feeling so very nervous? This was Simon, one of her oldest friends for goodness sake. She had loved him once, but he had never showed an interest in her; if anything, after meeting Robert, he distanced himself somewhat from her life.

As the car pulled up, she was shocked to see that he was sitting in the back, her bags stowed away in the boot, the chauffer opening the door for her. She slid herself in beside him, the cavern between them filled thankfully by the arm rest. Passing her a glass of champagne, the bubbles popping on her hand as she raised it to her lips.

"Cheers," he said, raising his in the air as they both sipped the cool liquid, its icy feel sliding down the back of her throat, made her shudder a little, and Simon broke the ice with a little laugh.

Lifting up the armrest, he reached out his hand and took her left hand in his. Raising it up to examine the mark that her wedding ring had left behind. He kissed her third finger ever so gently, sending a shudder through her body that was so unexpected it made Isabella gasp. Keeping hold of her hand, he winked at her and gently laid both their hands on the cool leather where they stayed entwined for the whole journey to Surrey.

"Hey, sleepyhead," Simon said as he reached over and gently nudged Isabella awake.

"Sorry, I have been so busy you should have woken me up."

"Never," he said with the sweetest smile she had ever seen. "Come on we are here and everything is ready for you."

His home was an old manor house in the Surrey countryside. Handed down through the generations, it was now his turn to inhabit its beautiful walls and make his own memories there.

The sight of the staircase leading to the galleried second floor took her breath away. She had been here years ago when his parents had lived there but it looked so very different now.

"Have you decorated?" she said, easing off her shoes before entering the splendour of it all. Her feet were killing her, and all she wanted to do was relax in a warm bath and put on something terribly comfortable.

As if he read her mind, he held out his hand and led her up the stairs and into a beautiful suite of rooms. She spotted the bath sitting in the centre of the second room instantly, steam rising from it and the scent of magnolia heightened her senses and made her smile.

"Is this for me?" she said, looking at Simon now. She feared he would see how very nervous she was around him all of a sudden if she made eye contact.

"Yes, take a dip. There are clean pyjamas and a gown, some fluffy slippers, and take your pick of the perfumes. I wasn't sure what you would like, so I bought the lot." he said, laughing a little. His nervousness too, ever there just below the surface.

Heading out of the room and down the stairs, he headed for the kitchen. Everything was ready as he had instructed, and the staff had taken their leave. The rest was up to him. As he headed towards his own suite on the ground floor, he prayed that everything that he had planned for the evening would be to Isabella's liking and would make her happy. He had spent the last three decades loving a woman that he had never had the nerve to tell in his youth. He wasn't going to let her go again, not if he could help it.

Having showered and donned the same matching pyjamas, robe and fluffy slippers, he headed towards the great room. His staff had laid out a picnic on the carpet, and as he put down some cushions and pillows for them to rest on, he scanned the room to make sure that everything was in place.

Fetching the champagne from the kitchen, its icy bucket dripping water as he walked it through the house. He was all set, as Isabella came down the stairs and smiled at hm, melting his heart and making it soar. He could see from the look in her eyes that she was ready.

Isabella searched his face as she walked over to where he was standing. Their matching outfits made her laugh a little, and he just shrugged.

"Wanted to make you feel at home," he said, taking her into his arms and kissing her gently at first and then with more passion than Isabella had felt in years. Both shaking ever so slightly with the built-up tension of thirty years between them.

"Why did you allow him to treat you that way?" he found himself saying.

"Shh,' Isabella said, her soothing words calming his anger, and as she kissed him back, she left no doubt in his mind that she wasn't going anywhere.

Book 2

Telford Parade – Whatever Next

Chapter 1

Feeling the coolness of the metal between her fingers, literally sending a shiver down her spine, after a few deep breaths, she unlocked the front door. Nester and her boys were about to take the first step into their new home. The pebble dashing, once vibrant and clean, showed its patches of emptiness; it had long since seen better days. The big, brown, wooden door, a fan of amber glass across the top, hinted at light as it swung open, offering up the next step for this brave family. The housing estate in Streatham was a far cry from the flat they had shared in Kennington: two rooms for all of them and nothing of substance inside.

With a rush of excitement, the boys were all but pushing their mum over. Joshua, his big yellow truck that Steven had given him, clutched under one arm, headed for the stairs. The carpet beneath his feet was a luxury he had never felt before, running from room to room, finding the one he was going to share with Samuel. Their wooden bunk beds already placed against the wall. The smell of fresh paint and new carpet making everything real.

Samuel, all thoughts of leaving his friends behind now gone, ran through the passageway and out into the kitchen. Its countertops clean and fresh, a kettle and toaster waiting for the morning rush, standing proudly on the side. The new cooker in the centre, a beacon of hope for happier times and home-cooked meals. A sheer wall of glass separating the dining area from the kitchen. Samuel could imagine his mum chatting to them as she prepared their food. The big wooden table, its benches reminding him of the school hall at lunchtime, making him smile. Chester and Kenny had found it in a flea market in Camden. Everyone had been so kind in offering to help once they knew who they were helping.

Chad, ever the protector, placed his hand into his mother's, and as they walked through the house, their eyes filled with tears of joy. His little hand squeezing hers, as they both knew they were finally home. Climbing the stairs, Chad found his tiny box room. Its built-in wardrobe and long white shelf was enough for him. His three Penguin Classic books (Animal Farm being his favourite) had been stashed in a bag as he left the flat; they would take pride of place in their new home. The Tottenham bedding he had longed for adorning his new single bed; what more could a nine-year-old boy want in life?

Staring in, Nester was scared to enter her beautiful big room; was it really all hers? Jenny, her best friend, had made sure everything was just so; the chintz curtains and bedspread, a splash of colour that made

Nester smile. Her friend knew her so well. As she walked around her new room, she imagined the Sunday mornings with all three boys scrambling into her bed for a cuddle; the chattering and the love, and the certainty of no more fear!

Once Chester and Steven had started the process of helping this fragile little family, everything had fallen into place. The endless interviews, statements, medical records and general prodding and poking into every area of their lives had culminated in this very moment. Never again would Darren Williams hurt them; they had made sure of that. He was going away for a very long time. Pressing charges and finally allowing people in to see what was happening was like a flood gate opening; Nester wished she had acted sooner.

Fear, Nester realised, was just an emotion; it had made her withdraw and assume that what she had was her lot. With the initial help from the people at the pub, and since then, her friend Jenny, the refuge and everyone else, they were now all able to believe in miracles. And as Chad always said, Steven was the Earth angel that came to save them all.

The bang on the front door stopped them in their tracks, the fear taking hold of them all. As Nester neared the window, the smile on her face told them everything was okay. Pulling up outside, she could see Chester climbing out of his car. Steven was already at the door, a small, elegant woman by his side; his companion for the day. Nester couldn't believe her eyes. A van was pulling up too. As the boys all ran towards the front door to open it, Steven all but fell through it.

"Hello boys, what do you think of your new home?" he said, trying to get himself heard over the din.

As the chattering got louder, Steven scooped Joshua up, carrying him under his arm, leading them all towards the sitting room. Elizabeth Summers followed him through the house, helping the removal people to place pieces of furniture where they made sense. A brown leather sofa; it had seen some action but still had a good lifetime ahead of it. Two big chairs, and a stylish coffee table that caused Chad to whistle through his teeth.

"Wow, Mum, is this all ours?" he said incredulously. As Nester nodded her head, her eyes seeking Stevens.

"Just a few things to get you started," he said with a smile. Her heart was fit to burst; was this really all theirs?

"Nester, this is Beth," Steven finally said as they bustled to and fro with boxes and bags. As the ladies hugged and the boys all looked on in wonder, Steven couldn't help but smile. Everything had fallen into place, and the best was yet to come.

"Tea, let's all have tea," Nester said after the removal people had taken the last bags up to the box room, filled with books and toys for Chad, even though he kept saying he didn't need anything. Chester knew how he loved books and had found a few more Penguin

Classics to add to his meagre collection. The large brown teddy bear, a relic from his own childhood, would be great company for this little boy in his new single bed. Kenny had even thrown in his beloved Tottenham scarf for good measure; after all, he never went to games anymore now that his dad had stopped calling.

As the chatter died down, everyone sat and pondered this splendid new home.

It was Nester who broke the silence, "Thank you all for coming today and helping us move, it's been so lovely having you all here."

As Beth cleared her throat, she knew she had to say this without sounding patronising; for Nester was a proud woman and not keen on charity. But she knew that these new friends were doing what was best for her and her boys.

"I wanted to be a part of today because I am hoping that you, Nester, and the boys, of course will be able to help me with a little venture that myself and Jessica, Steven's fiancée, are embarking on. It's going to take some hard work and determination on all of our parts, but I think you will be a perfect fit. We are hoping you will say yes to becoming our new centre manager." All but spitting out her tea, Nester couldn't believe her ears.

"Yes, yes, and yes again!" she said, the tears streaming down her face, smiling now as she realised why Steven had been so insistent on her taking those free ICT courses at the local library. This had to be by far the best day of her life.

As the boys all jumped up and down, whooping and wailing. Nester and Beth took themselves off into the kitchen to clean up and make another cuppa.

"I can't thank you enough," Nester said as she passed a large white mug to Beth, who was standing tea towel poised. "You know, this is all new to me, and in so many ways, we need each other. One day I will share my story, but for today we are celebrating, even if it is only with tea." As the two ladies laughed and busied themselves, the boys had long since retreated to their new rooms, leaving Chester and Steven to ponder the day. What a day it had been.